D1330861

PRAISE FOR *BEʌ*

'Brilliant. *Bent* compellingly re-imagines a shocki

 **libraries**

Baillieston Library
141 Main Street
Glasgow G69 6AA
Phone: 0141 276 0706

WITHDRAWN

This book is due for return on or before the last date shown below. It may be renewed by telephone, personal application, fax or post, quoting this date, author, title and the book number.

Glasgow Life and its service brands, including Glasgow Libraries, (found at www.glasgowlife.org.uk) are operating names for Culture and Sport Glasgow.

Glasgow
CITY COUNCIL

'Perhaps
Harold ' 'rious copper of the postwar era,
contradi...or has taken many literary guises, his
nicked, ' presence and catchphrase "You're
and Jake cling its way into work by Joe Orton
turned ' has delved so deeply into what
whose a AS into a peacetime detective
epithet o" led to ignominy and the
braved n – *Bent* – until Joe Thomas
Challen... then de...ectively channelling
author he events that forged and
rilliant' **Cathi Unsworth,**

'Had J... *d Penny Blues*

a corru...
this. B... rated on a novel about
Willet...tten something like
my memory' **Paul**
e Look of Love

...ing
...ur ...
...lowi...
...'s nee...
...us viol...
...oughtfu...

...y

...bunking o...
...it and veg...
...wick Street ...
...ach, then to t...
...llowed by a n...
...ent. Shoot off ...
...ck up for an all-...
...y-eyed. We were ...
...t times. Not bent
...**of the Sharman no**...

PRAISE FOR THE SÃO PAULO QUARTET

'Thomas's fine series offers a wonderfully vivid introduction to a society in violent, vibrant flux' *Mail on Sunday* **Thriller of the month**

'Great crime fiction hinges on a sense of place, and in his sophisticated debut, Thomas proves an adroit guide to a city that has developed at dizzying speed' *GQ*

'With its feverish energy, opulent nightlife, culture and chaos, the Brazilian megalopolis is a perfect setting for Joe Thomas's crime thrillers' *Guardian*

'As vibrant, colourful and complex as South America's largest city' *Irish Independent*

'Stylish, sharp-witted and taut. A must for modern noir fans' *NB Magazine*

'A new and distinct voice in crime fiction of the city' **Susanna Jones, author of** *The Earthquake Bird*

'Fresh, gripping and incredibly assured' **Stav Sherez, author of** *The Intrusions*

ABOUT THE AUTHOR

Joe Thomas is the author of *Paradise City, Gringa* and *Playboy*. The final part in his São Paulo quartet, *Brazilian Psycho*, is scheduled for publication in autumn 2020. *Bent* is his first London novel.

ALSO BY JOE THOMAS

Paradise City

Gringa

Playboy

BENT

BENT
Joe Thomas

A

Arcadia Books Ltd
139 Highlever Road
London W10 6PH

www.arcadiabooks.co.uk

First published in the United Kingdom 2020
Copyright © Joe Thomas 2020

Joe Thomas has asserted his moral right to be identified as the authors of this
work in accordance with the Copyright, Designs and Patents Act, 1988.

All Rights Reserved. No part of this publication may be reproduced in any
form or by any means without the written permission of the publishers.

A catalogue record for this book is available from the British Library.

ISBN 978-1-911350-73-6

Typeset in Garamond by MacGuru Ltd
Printed and bound by TJ International, Padstow PL28 8RW

ARCADIA BOOKS DISTRIBUTORS ARE AS FOLLOWS:

in the UK and elsewhere in Europe:
BookSource
50 Cambuslang Road
Cambuslang
Glasgow G32 8NB

in USA/Canada:
BookMasters
Baker & Taylor
30 Amberwood Parkway
Ashland, OH 44805
USA

in Australia/New Zealand:
NewSouth Books
University of New South Wales
Sydney NSW 2052

BENT

Author's note

During the Second World War, my grandfather, Ronald 'Bob' Young, served in 2SAS with Harold Challenor, most notably in Operation Wallace, behind enemy lines in France in 1944. Like Challenor, after the war, he became a policeman, though his career was markedly different.

I grew up with stories of the exploits of my grandfather and Challenor, and other men like them. My brother, sister and I would listen, rapt, wide-eyed, to the tales our grandfather and his friends would tell us. Our grandmother, too: she was the real storyteller. It was an important part of our childhood.

Although based on historical events and involving historical figures, *Bent* is a work of fiction, and certain names, dates, places, organisations have been changed for dramatic purposes. A bibliography follows the main text together with a list of quoted material.

Harold Challenor is a controversial figure; this novel is an imagined version of part of his life.

In memory of my grandparents, Mary and Ronald 'Bob' Young; and for their great-grandson, Lucian

With a few more Challenors, the war would have been over sooner
Major Roy Farran

Come not between the dragon and his wrath
Shakespeare, *King Lear*

Hero

The first time I met Harold Challenor, he frisked me for weapons –
I was ten years old.

It's quite a story, the life of Detective Sergeant Harold 'Tanky'
Challenor.

He and my grandad served together in 2SAS in the Second
World War.

Challenor was a war hero, a copper, a storyteller, a lover, a
lunatic, and a whole lot more.

He was the scourge of Soho, that 'mad bastard' Challenor.

The Kray twins offered a grand to anyone who'd help stitch him
up.

But that's a mere footnote.

This story, it's all true, all of it.

The Trial

The Old Bailey
June 1964

Challenor sits. Challenor waits. He sits on a bench outside the courtroom at the Old Bailey, and waits to give his testimony. The Old Bailey, he thinks. In the dock. Here we go. *Here we fucking go.*

There's a young police constable sat next to him, keeping an eye, that's all. Making sure. No bolters in this court, no runners, not on your –

You know the word: *life.* No runners, no way, not on your life, son.

The lad says, 'You done it then?' He winks.

Cheeky sod, Challenor thinks. Did I do it? Well, did I do *what,* young man?

He says, 'Listen, my young beauty, you keep your trap shut.'

Challenor smiles. The lad smiles back. The hallway clock makes its noise. They both listen. They can't hear nothing else. They can't hear nothing else from inside. From inside the courtroom.

Did I do it? *Did I do it?*

Challenor sits. Challenor waits. He sits and waits and thinks about this question. He fingers the piece of paper he has in his pocket:

If you can wait and not be tired by waiting,
Or being lied about, don't deal in lies.

He's not sure.

Did I do *what*, old chum? he thinks.

Less of the old, eh.

There was a letter. From that quack down by the river. Sargent was his name. A Dr Sargent, psychiatrist.

Quite something, that letter, evidence-wise:

I am certain that Harold Challenor is very mad indeed.

It said, among some other things.

Indeed.

Did I do it? Did I do *what*, my old son?

Challenor sits and waits and his thoughts turn to Doris. There's a lot he can forgive himself, he thinks, but letting her down, letting down his wife, is certainly not one of them.

He wonders if he already has done.

Part One

WHO DARES WINS

July 1962–December 1962

One

———

*'A big showdown for power is coming and when
it does come it will be a bloody battle.'*

Challenor scarfs prawn dumplings. He wolfs brown ale. He's sat at
the counter of the Chinaman's copper-friendly crab shack on Lisle
Street, Chinatown. This place was set up by Brilliant Chang, Chan
Nan, the first oriental gangster to run the roost in these fine parts
– then cut the roost's neck and sell it in a pancake.

Brilliant Chang didn't last long. Show-off, he was, no discretion.
Did a fourteen stretch for drug trafficking, then was stuck straight
back on the long-haul junk across the ocean for home.

Challenor is off-duty happy and gulping beer. He eyes the calendar: Year of the Tiger. He slurps a bowl of noodle soup.

He nods at the Chinaman. 'What year are you?' he asks.

The Chinaman smiles. 'Year of the Rat.' He gestures at the room,
the kitchen. 'Why we don't have a pest problem. Only room for one.'
The Chinaman laughs hard. 'The elegant way you're applying yourself
to the chow, friend,' he says, 'I'm guessing you're a different animal.'

'I fear a punchline,' Challenor says.

The Chinaman grins. 'I'll leave you to think about it.'

Challenor checks the calendar.

1922: Year of the Dog. Well-played.

The Chinaman's back. 'How's the Mad House?' he asks.

'Busy,' Challenor says.

———

The Mad House. West End Central. The busiest nick in London, CID, and Challenor's base. Covers Mayfair and Soho. Brass don't let him anywhere near Mayfair.

'Well, you've a rum crowd putting the bite on in these parts, Harry. You deserve a promotion, boy.' The Chinaman looks around. 'Here, you know what?' he says. 'You could eat in a better place than this, that's for sure.' He points at Challenor's brown ale. 'One for the road? On the house, mind.'

Challenor smiles, shakes his head.

'Suit yourself.' The Chinaman floats off to drink the health of some other punter.

It's all God's honest, of course, Challenor thinks. Soho at the end of the 50s was a jungle. The Street Offences act of '59 saw to that. No more women of the night on the public prowl; all behind the clubs now. And the clubs all a front. Italian Albert Dimes saw off poor old Jewish Jack 'bother' Spot with a razor. He found himself in a spot all right, that night. The Kosher King fucked off sharpish after that. And it's gone from there, Challenor thinks. Ronnie Knight at the A&R on Charing Cross Road; the Krays at the Stragglers, off Cambridge Circus.

And that's why I'm here, he thinks –

Detective Sergeant Harold 'Tanky' Challenor.

What's a couple of wide-boy thugs to an ex-SAS paratrooper?

Challenor wipes his mouth. He sees off the rest of his brown ale. He throws coins on the counter.

Challenor's off duty, but he's never *off* duty. He wraps up in a long, summer coat. Not the most subtle of disguises, but it'll do.

What are you *going to do about it?*

Challenor means business. He doesn't mess about, Challenor.

He's following Flying Squad Rule no. 1: catch the jokers at it.

That way you can always sus them, bring them in on a possible, a charge.

Red-handed is stone-cold cell time, Challenor's learnt *that* rule well enough.

And you have to get up pretty early, as the saying goes, to catch the poxy bastards round West End Central way.

He's out the Chinaman's place, turns right down Lisle Street. He glances at the knocking shop on the corner, a sign, 'Models', on an open door. Not the most subtle of disguises.

He crosses Shaftesbury Avenue, and shuffles along Dean Street aiming for Wilf Gardiner's place, the Geisha club, on Moor Street, just off Cambridge Circus. He keeps his head down as he passes the French House. He's heard there are a couple of faces about and he doesn't want anybody the wiser regarding this little off-duty jaunt. Research trip, he's calling it.

The Geisha club, Challenor thinks.

Not the most subtle of disguises.

Old Wilf Gardiner is no sweetheart, Challenor knows this. Convictions for violence, dishonesty. He tuned up a traffic warden not long ago, and his strip clubs are rife with solicitation, short-time brass in upstairs rooms and whatnot. No, he is not a very nice chap at all, old Wilf Gardiner, and it strikes Challenor now that it's an unlikely set of circumstances that has led them to become something like accomplices.

He's passed the Three Greyhounds on the corner of Moor and Old Compton, and it's quiet in there, this early-afternoon booze slot isn't too busy, no, but he keeps himself to himself, doesn't call out to Luciano – Lucky Luke – owner of his favourite Italian canteen, his very favourite trattoria, to be precise, Limoncello, across the road, like he sometimes does. He wants to know what exactly it is Wilf wants –

Yes, it seems that old Wilf Gardiner is having a spot of.

A week before, Challenor is at Wilf's other place, the Phoenix.

9

'I'm telling you, Harry, these fuckers are taking the right old Mick,' Wilf says.

Challenor sits and listens. He swallows beer.

'They're round the Geisha early July, right,' old Wilf is saying, 'and Ford – that's Johnnie Ford, yeah, local face, a decent-looking lad I'll give him that, a two-bob villain sort, you know him, course you do – so this Ford has told me to hire some of his mob, you know, working, bar staff, delivery lackeys, that kind of thing. Except their jobs will be on the books, but they ain't gonna be punching in, know what I mean? So you see where this is going.'

Challenor does see. *Protection.*

'So I've told him we could talk about it, and he's told me no, no discussion. And that I need to watch where I walk and watch every way.'

'And?'

'They fancy coming back and giving me a belting,' Wilf says. 'Same day I've come across him and a couple of his monkeys on Charing Cross Road and he's butted me, and I've struck him, and it's got a touch tasty, but I reckoned that'd be the end.'

'But it wasn't.'

'No.'

The following day young Ford and his mate Riccardo Pedrini head over to the Phoenix for a pow-wow to square things.

'Giving up on protection then, are you?' Old Wilf says, smirking.

Ford grins, and turns, and does one. Scarpers.

Pedrini points his finger at Old Wilf and says, 'You try and get Johnnie Ford nicked, and I will cut you up.' He turns away. Turns back. 'And I get nicked for that, my lover, I'll get out and cut you up again.'

'Yes, darling,' Wilf says. And he winks, and he heads in, head high.

Pride comes before one, and blah blah blah and all that jazz,

Challenor thinks now, as he heads towards the Geisha. Course it's not the charming Italian waiter Pedrini that Challenor wants. He's just a wannabe with a blade who's known Ford for donkeys. And Ford is a cutthroat chancer who won't last.

No, Challenor's after bigger fish, and he's using Old Wilf here to lure them out of the weeds and into clear, running water.

Challenor's after a certain racketeer named Joseph Francis Oliva. King Oliva.

*

You're itching. You're drunk and you're itching. Algeria, 1942, and fuck all happening. Punch-ups with Yanks in the bars. Lying around getting a soldier's suntan, itching and waiting.

You're drunk in a bar.

'So you're an orderly?'

You hear: oi-duh-ly.

You grunt.

'What's that, a nurse?'

You hear: a noi-ss.

Smack. Have that, you Yank cunt. You turn. Plant your bonce on his pal. Crunch. And we're off. Glass smashes. Cheers. Head down, fists up. In seconds, tables crash. You pick up a chair leg and turn. Then whistles, shouts, cheering, laughter.

Military Police, or some Yank nonsense.

'Nah, it was nothing, was it, Harry? Just a laugh, guv.'

Nods. Hands raised, drinks gathered, sipped. Your Yank pals grinning. Yeah, have that. You grin back. MPs fuck off out of it, and you shake hands with your new friends, clap their backs.

'What the fuck is a noi-ss?' you say.

You all get good and drunk, brothers in arms and all that.

If you want something enough, you'll get it. *You repeat the phrase to yourself again and again:* if you want something enough, you'll get it. *And you want it, all right. This medical orderly business is not what you signed up for. Held in reserve, attached to the First Army, just a mass of bodies and equipment to keep Rommel from heading east while Monty cleared El Alamein.*

Least the booze is cheap. Algiers, cheers; cheers, Algiers. Every night you're cracking that gag, toasting the sky and the sand. Bored out your skull. Not what you signed up for.

Then, things change for you: a touch. Young Randolph Churchill, son of Big Winston, rolls into the camp looking for likely lads for 62 Commando. You're straight in there like a Yank desert rat up an Algiers whore. They like the look of you. And you're in. There's a catch: you have to remain an orderly. An oi-duh-ly. Fuck. But you do all the drills, all the training, you're top marks across the board, the most aggressive oi-duh-ly the Commandos ever had.

And before too long, you're in, you're fully fledged, and it's on.

You have no fear of death; if you die, a whole fucking bunch of their mob is going with you.

'Where's your cap, orderly?' An officer asks you.

It's a good question. You've lost yours, and the famous Green Berets ain't turned up yet.

'You'll have to wear this, Tanky.'

The officer hands you an old Tank Corps hat.

Tanky. Now you're Tanky.

*

Challenor shuffles on towards the Geisha club. He grimaces, growls to himself.

There are quacks after him, talking about him, doctors, you know, *that* lot –

Psychiatrists.

They're giving it the Battle Fatigue, the Combat Stress Reaction. Brass at head office are worried about Challenor, want him examined, assessed.

Course, he's got form, Challenor.

His childhood was what you'd call peripatetic, he thinks now, you know, if you wanted to give it a positive spin, a *gloss*. His old man had to uproot the family time and again, what with the bailiffs and bookies and landlords and whatnot always calling, all hours. Late-night-run-for-it type of thing. Challenor and his sister, sleepy-eyed in the boot of the car, meagre possessions packed around them.

It was only when Challenor's old man got a job at Leavesden Mental Hospital in Hertfordshire that they had any sort of stability. He was a nurse, which is a laugh, considering the little care he ever showed at home.

'You're a mistake, boy, you got that?'

Was the kind of thing.

Challenor got a job there too, which he admits smacks of a bit odd, but there was a characteristic bit of his own dodgy logic to it. The young bachelors, your single male nurses, got lodgings there to sweeten the deal.

So it was a way out of home.

It definitely smacks of a bit odd, Challenor knows this, when you consider the contempt with which Challenor holds his old man, this father in name alone who let himself succumb to drink, and who expressed his own brand of contempt, of fury, with his fists.

Mean, sadistic, cruel, a tyrant – are a few words Challenor's used.

Taking this job got Challenor away from those furies, those rages, those fists.

He would aim low, Challenor's old man, no visible marks.

He didn't fancy giving young Harry a belting in public, so that was that.

Not so much as following in his footsteps as getting out from under his shadow.

Course, the institutional experience, the medical experience Challenor gathers there, is considered invaluable when he signs up.

So he's not a soldier, frustratingly, but a medical orderly.

Boy from Watford, a drinker and skirt chaser, in the Royal Army Medical Corps.

Which doesn't last long, of course.

Don't let Brass fob you off, Challenor thinks now. You're Tanky, boy.

What are you going to do about it, eh?

Box it, that's what, *shelve* it, that's what I'll do, Challenor thinks, what I've done every day, I'll box it, I'll *shelve* it.

So he does.

He ducks down the stairs of Wilf Gardiner's Geisha club.

Here we go, he thinks. *Here we go.*

*

You're boxed in tight on a submarine, hammock-bound, discussing the weight and the length and the depth of the pop of the explosives you've got stashed below you in an odd-looking tin fish. Submarine's name: Safari. You're on fucking safari, old chum. First mission: Marigold – 2SAS to connect with an agent nearby on the Sardinian coast and take a prisoner. What you do with that prisoner is what you're looking forward to: interrogation to ascertain German strength in Sardinia pre-launch of Operation Husky, the Allied invasion of Sicily.

You're in, lad. It is all on.

But it's high summer and the daylight hours are long, so you and yours are submerged for very, very long periods. And the air is close, and there ain't much of it, and you're struggling a little, and the smell, the smell, it's, you know the word, pungent, *an acrid, fetid stink, but you can't complain, oh no sir, Tanky can't complain. And your new mate Ronald 'Bob' Young has been awfully quiet for some time, and you know the lad don't like confined spaces, so you comfort yourself with being a staunch companion. You comfort yourself by comforting him. You like Bob; you trained together. Now it's end of May '43, and here you are.*

It's a long five days you do, down there. You think of slave ships. You think of wombs. You think of coffins and graves, buried alive. You think of Doris.

You try not to think.

And then you arrive for Marigold part deux. The senior 2SAS lieutenant types have done their bit, dropping off a notebook or some other posh-gentleman spy palaver in some cloak and dagger business, and now it's your turn. The Safari *surfaces and periscopes about for quite some time. Bob is happier. Neither of you is really much happier. Waiting, you begin to realise, is worse than combat. Why? You, and Bob, and the rest of your mob, ain't scared of death, no sir, you're all scared of disfigurement, of some disabling injury that fucks you back to Blighty on a stretcher, half-life, half-lived and fucked royally in the name of the King. No, you're not worried about death. But this waiting while the Navy checks on your landing spot –*

Deathly slow.

You're on the top of the Safari *and you're foot-pumping the dinghies. Foot-pumping the buggers! Well, apparently, the compressed air bottles that'd fill 'em in moments are emergencies only. Fair dos. But Christ on a bike, the air feels, the air feels* good *up here!*

'Gulp that down, Tanky!' Bob says, grinning, his face red, his ears red, his mouth in and out as his foot goes up and down.

'Gulp on, mate.' You smile. 'Gulp on!'

And the pair of you gulp to fuck, you do.

Then you're in the dinghies and the current's against you, and the landing spot is all submerged rocks, and the lot of you are realising that fuck, you're in blow-up kids' boats to take on the German army some-where close to Italy, and the submarine has orders to bugger off if you're not back in time, and you ghost into a beach cove that was absolutely not on the menu, but there ain't nothing you can hear, and you've not said a word for two hours or so, just followed who's leading, and then you're on the shingle shore, and how the fuck do you approach quiet like, in boots on a shingle shore?

We going to have to paddle back to Algiers then?

What are you going to do about that, *my son?*

And then, all the worry about boots on shale, and there's a clatter of steel on stone, rifles dropped, and then all hell let loose, and machine guns and small arms fire is coming at you like a rush of light in the pitch dark, and then the cunts light a flare, and you're down hard but really you know you're a duck in a barrel and how the fuck do you get out of this one?

But you know what? You ain't scared. The bullets are flying well above. They're mob-handed, but they don't know where the fuck you are.

And that's the SAS in a fucking phrase, my old darling –

You know; they don't.

Wait for the order –

Head down, and –

Wait.

*

Challenor orders a brown ale and waits for old Wilf.

King Oliva, he thinks.

Oliva's been around for some time, protection racketeer, and Challenor knows *all* about him. Course he does. Everyone does. King Oliva –

Press hero.

The Daily Sketch, 30 June 1959.
Here he is, Challenor thinks, remembering the piece.
All of him in an interview.
He's read the piece. He *knows* the piece.
King Oliva. Wallflower. Mug. Show-off –
He's certainly something.

JOSEPH FRANCIS OLIVA, aged 19, of 6 Ratcliffe Buildings, Bourne Estate, Clerkenwell, N. says:

I was shot in the chest as I stood in the doorway of Carlo's Restaurant, Theobalds Road, Holborn, last night.

I am a Roman Catholic, educated at St Peter's Italian School in Clerkenwell Road, leaving at 15. Since then I have had four convictions – one at 15 for stealing a car; another at 16 for stealing a motor cycle; three years borstal reduced to six months on appeal for breaking and entering at 18, at 17 I was fined for causing grievous bodily harm.

I was used to be a fish porter but I have not worked for two years.

My father is a docker and I have two brothers, aged 22 and 29. The eldest one is married.

In the shooting last night I got about 16 lead shots in my chest. My mates picked them out with a knife.

This is what happened. Ten of us were drinking tea when a black Austin pulled up outside the café. A man stuck a single barrel shotgun through the window when I went out to see them. When I was two yards from the car, the man fired. The car raced off before I could get at the man. I am not disclosing his name to anyone, not even the police. I know who he is and I am out to get him myself. I will settle this my way.

I went to the Homeopathic Hospital. They gave me an injection but I insisted on leaving. My mates had washed the wounds and picked out the 16 shots. Perhaps there are one or two still in but this doesn't worry me.

The reason for the shooting is because I am the leader of a gang 400 strong. They call me King Oliva.

The shooting is in retaliation for a fight which took place in a dice speiler in a Camden Town club three weeks ago. It was a revenge attack because six of us cleaned up all the money, about £80. We just did it to show I was the "Guvnor". The money has gone on a car – a big Buick car, big enough to hold a lot of us.

I am going to be boss of the nightclubs – and run the nightclubs around the West End. I have got to shift one or two big gang leaders to do it. But I have got a man behind me financing me. I already work for him. We have got to have cars to get around in and "clobber" (clothes) to look the part.

We already get a nice little living from the East End clubs and some in the West End. And we look after about 12 clubs. We see no one takes liberties with the juke boxes and we make sure there is no trouble in the clubs. The club owners pay us for this and we give the money to the "Governer". He is a London businessman who owns property and lives in a big house on the outskirts of town.

I command about 400 people. I can get them all at just 24 hours' notice just by fifteen to twenty phone calls to individual top men in each gang. Then I am the Guvnor of them all. They are different gangs from all North and South London but mostly in the Theobalds Road area.

All the 400 do not get paid. They do it for the kicks. They are all teenagers. They worship me – King Oliva.

We last called the 400 up six months ago for a big fight at the Memorial Hall, Camden Town. But the other side backed out.

I have two Lieutenants. I split equally with them. I am drawing about £30 a week at the moment.

We do not value our lives

because without money we are nothing.

I am not worried about jail. If you do these things you have to expect "bird". It is one of those things. I am not afraid of prison or afraid of anything or anybody. When I am dead, that's it.

I am going to be boss because there are rich pickings. All a fellow needs is guts and backing – and I've got both. We are going to live good with cars, and fine clothes. A big showdown for power is coming and when it does come it will be a bloody battle.

I used to fight for fun but now I'm going to the top for money. Girls? I go out with a few but I don't go steady. I've not time for them in my business.

(Signed) JOSEPH OLIVA

Challenor considers:

We do not value our lives because without money we are nothing.
It ricochets –
What are you going to do about it?
Business.

My business. Challenor knows business all right. Challenor knows life. Challenor knows value. He's been there, at the business end. Life-wise.

He *knows*, all right. *When I am dead, that's it.* Challenor understands –

He's never been afraid of death.

*

You wait. Your head down. Your mate Bob next to you. The beach cutting up, opening up around you both. You sit tight. You sit tight, and you wait for your orders.

'When we next get home,' Bob says, 'I'm asking Mary to marry me. Honest woman and whatnot.'

You laugh. 'You soppy bugger,' you say. 'You're only saying that now we're being shot at.'

Bob smiles. 'Either way,' he says.

You laugh again. You're not afraid of death. You're not afraid. And you wait. The onslaught seems to fade. You're going to get out of this, you think. This bit, anyway. And you think of Doris, she's what pops in, first thought, first sign of relief.

Doris.

Honest woman and whatnot.

You can do that.

Bob can, you can.

*

'So why am I here, Wilf?' Challenor asks.

Challenor nurses his brown ale. Not really drinking it, not really, but not *not* drinking it.

The Geisha is known for its brown ale, after all, so you might as well, you know, have one, the one, just the one. It *is* known for it, its brown ale, after all.

'Updates, Harry, updates,' Gardiner says. 'Progress, or change, or both.' He looks around the club, quiet in the post-lunch slump, the girls listless, nap-ready. 'Stuff you should know about, Harry, that's why you're here.'

Challenor doesn't like Gardiner. Nobody likes Gardiner, in fact.

Radio's on. The news. Something about a riot in Birmingham. Darkies having a pop at the local constabulary, Challenor thinks. Sounds tasty. Don't blame them, to be fair. Give them credit, eh? It *does* them credit, after all, what with what goes on.

'Well?'

'You enjoying your brown ale, Harry?'

'I'm not here for the brown ale, Wilf.'

Gardiner nods and looks at Challenor in a way that makes Challenor feel that he, Challenor, has just made a very profound comment, of sorts. Like he's worked out some fiendishly difficult thing, had an insight, maybe, or an epiphany, even. Like he's really understood the Geisha club, and its purpose, or his purpose for being there.

What a muppet this Gardiner is, Challenor thinks.

'What I mean is, Harry,' Gardiner says, 'is that I want you to come upstairs with me, out the back. I want to show you something.' He gestures at the bottle of beer. 'But I certainly do *not* want to interrupt your enjoyment of our famous brown ale.' He smiles. 'It is, after all, what we're famous for. You know what I mean?'

Challenor groans, and smiles. He mutters, 'Christ.'

Challenor picks up the bottle and empties it down his throat. It is good, after all, this brown ale. Really thirst-quenching, as they, you know, as they *say*.

Radio's playing Roses are Red. Doris likes this one. Bobby Vinton, Polack crooner. Yeah, sugar is sweet, all right, Challenor thinks. Not as sweet as you though, old son.

Challenor smiles. 'Lead on, Wilf, lead on. I'm all yours.'

They walk down a filthy basement corridor. Challenor knows this corridor will take them up into a cramped garage behind Old Compton and Greek. They climb the staircase at the back of the club, at the end of the filthy corridor, beyond the office, behind the door that says 'Staff Only' on it, just right of where the girls get ready to do their bit. Not so much a dressing room as a dressing down. Challenor sees the way the wallpaper is curled and tatty, *peeling*, the wear in the carpet, the *balding* carpet.

'Where's the glamour, eh, Wilf? Where's the glamour of a night out in Soho *gone*, eh?' Challenor says.

Gardiner snorts. 'Change, Harry,' he says, 'all change round here.' He stops and jerks his thumb at the street. 'All about the long hairs and the shagging now, Harry. Rhythm and blues, my old son. You heard it?'

Challenor shakes his head.

'Had a band on at the Marquee a couple of weeks ago,' Gardiner says, 'playing rhythm and blues. Their first gig. Moody buggers, they were. The singer looks like a bird. Rolling Stones, I believe they're called.'

'Oh yeah?' Challenor says.

'Oh *yeah*,' Gardiner says. 'You should have seen the tarts. They were *pissing* themselves. A whole mob of teenage tarts *pissing* themselves.'

Gardiner gestures to a door that leads out into an alley, and then to a tiny parking space. 'Yep,' he says, 'rhythm and blues. It's the future, Harry. Darkie Yank music played by grumpy white boys.' Gardiner opens the door and steps through. 'Pissing themselves, they were, the *tarts*.'

Challenor follows.

'It's the future, Harry. You mark my words. The future.'

Challenor marks his words and keeps an eye. The alley stinks of piss. There'll be a car at the end of it, he thinks, and they amble towards where it'd be parked.

'My Spanish mate Fat Juan took me,' Gardiner says, chuckling. 'Pissing themselves, they were.' He shakes his head. 'Old Fat Juan thought he'd died and gone to heaven.'

Fat Juan is neither fat nor Spanish. He's a rake-thin Colombian drug smuggler with a libido to match. A serious eye for – what he likes to call in his Latin tongue – the *putas*. Oh yes, he likes a bird, does Fat Juan. And he's not particular. Never let a day go by without Juan, is the joke, they say, back home, you know, *translated*. A regular down Walker's Court and upstairs on Peter Street. Challenor likes Fat Juan even less than he likes Old Wilf Gardiner.

They call him Fat Juan 'cos that's what he's got, they say, the women of the night, the *putas*: a fat one. Fat Juan and his fat one –

Challenor's skin crawls –

Poor slags, he thinks, and not for the first time.

What are you going to do about it?

What are you –

Challenor stops. He eyeballs Gardiner. 'He out, is he?' he asks. 'Fat Juan?'

'This way, Harry,' Gardiner says. 'Down here.'

*

The order is given: turn around, we're getting out. And hold fire –

They'll pinpoint our position if you carry on, so fucking stop.

You're disappointed, you are, you were itching to have a crack, but you see the logic of the experienced soldier, your senior officer, Sergeant Fitzpatrick.

So it's back to the dinghies.

'Head down, Bob,' you say, as you're crawling along the beach towards the inflatables.

There's Butch, close to you, shaking, shaken, the third member of your dinghy crew. Butch says nothing, and you grab his elbow and keep crawling.

You wade out in the darkness, the water cold and dark, an immense, cold, dark ocean, and you and Bob and Butch are trying to hop aboard this blow-up kids' boat, with bullets flying past, bouncing like skimming stones, and you're going to paddle this blow-up toy across the immense, cold, dark ocean, you are –

'That way,' Bob says, taking a position using his watch and the stars, and pointing. 'Head down this line.'

The bullets don't stop skimming across the cold, dark water.

'Put your backs into it,' Bob hisses.

But you don't make much progress, and the bullets skim, and the water seems darker and colder and more immense, and the blow-up dinghy seems even less suited to this frankly impossible-seeming task of finding the HMS Safari.

'They'll have gone, by now, surely,' Bob says, checking his watch again. 'Could be a long night.'

But you're still not getting very far. Circling, you are, it feels.

Then you realise, and you laugh, you look at Butch, and you realise and you laugh.

'Shut it, Tanky,' Bob hisses, again. 'What on earth is so fucking funny?'

'Turn round, Butch,' you say, and you grab him and pull him to you. 'He's all back to front, paddling the wrong way, the doofus,' you laugh. 'That's why we were going round and round in circles.'

'Jesus,' Bob says.

And you all shift positions, musical chairs, bit of pantomime, and still circles –

You laugh. You realise you've all just shifted and old Butch is still paddling against you. Again you laugh.

And the bullets are skimming, and the water is dark, and cold, and immense, and HMS Safari *has likely fucked off, and you're laughing, you're laughing, as your blow-up goes round in circles –*

*

The alley stinks of piss.

'You should clean this place up a bit, Wilf,' Challenor says. 'Whole place stinks of piss.'

'That's good advice, Harry,' Gardiner says. 'You ought to think about coming in with me, partners, like.'

Challenor ignores this.

'Then again,' Gardiner goes on, 'not *technically* my responsibility, this piss-stinking alley, is it?'

Challenor looks up. The sun has got his hat on. The air is thick with smoke and noise. The buildings either side of this piss-stinking alley are offices, and the odd residential, and, no doubt, the odd front. Their windows are grimy. Dark shapes move about behind some of them, but they're not very peeping Tom friendly, that's for sure. Perhaps the point, Challenor thinks. There are clouds swimming – front-*crawling* – through the blue sky towards Charing Cross Road.

They come to the car.

'Let's have it then, Wilf,' Challenor says. 'I'm not here for you to show off your motor, now am I?'

And it *is* a nice motor, Challenor thinks. He can't help himself. 'This new, Wilf?'

'Oof,' Gardiner says, 'this is the future, Harry.'

'I thought rhythm and blues was the future, Wilf.'

'Context, Harry, context.' Gardiner runs his hand over his motor like he's smoothing a blanket. 'October, mate, Earl's Court Motor Show, this little lovely will feature, you mark my words, Harry.'

'Oh yeah?'

'Oh *yeah*.' Gardiner's nodding, vigorously, staring wistfully at his motor. '48th British International Motor Show, half a million people from all over Europe, so they'll have this on display for your wops and your frogs and your dagos, and you won't be able to fucking parallel park on the Riviera for them, you mark them, Harry.'

Challenor's nodding too.

Gardiner goes on. 'Look at it, Harry. Ford Zephyr 4, Mark III. Four because it's got a four cylinder, which is the minimum welly a man should require, in my humble. Mine's got transmission, too. Automatic, obviously, I'm not a mug.'

Challenor's not sure about this.

'Look at the lines, Harry, the *colour*.'

It's sky blue, Challenor sees, and looks up. It matches this bright, sunny day, Gardiner's motor does.

'The Krauts will be pissing themselves when they see it, Harry. Perfect for an Autobahn, it is, a motor like this.'

Gardiner's caressing the motor's lines, running a single finger along these exquisite lines.

'Look at the way it turns up a touch at the back, a notch on the sides, mark, Harry, the positioning of the wing mirrors. This car is something, that's for sure.' Gardiner pauses. 'It's the future. Mark my words, they'll all be in them, the jet set, on the continent, after Earl's Court in October.'

'I don't doubt it, Wilf.'

Gardiner turns. 'So you understand, Harry, now I've said all this, quite how upset I am about what happened yesterday.'

Challenor nods. 'Go on.'

Gardiner opens the passenger door. He gestures for Challenor to look inside. Challenor leans in. He can see that the front seats have been sliced and shredded with a thick knife, a hunting knife, Challenor thinks. He looks in the back. The back seats have also been sliced and shredded with what looks like a hunting knife, a hefty blade, the sort that leaves quite the lacerations to whatever it is applied. There is a message, it appears, scrawled in what looks like lipstick around the lacerations on the sliced and shredded back seats.

The message, if Challenor is reading it correctly, states:

YOU

This scene moves Challenor. He is moved a little more than he would have expected, he realises.

'You can see, Harry, now,' Gardiner says, 'quite why I am so upset.'

'They've made a mess, Wilf, I'll give you that,' Challenor says.

'You know what it means, don't you?' Gardiner asks.

'I do, Wilf, yes.'

There are two messages here, Challenor thinks.

First message is –

We can get in your car and not leave any signs of a break-in

Second message is –

You don't do what we say, and we're going to cut you up

'You can see why I'm quite so upset, can't you, Harry?'

Riccardo Pedrini. Johnnie Ford –

King Oliva.

This is very likely their handiwork, Challenor thinks. Pedrini's threat to old Wilf Gardiner, Challenor knows all about.

What are you *going to do about it?*

This is their signature, all right. He's heard their plea, their defence, in the past. He's heard what they'd say, if he got hold of them now –

'A big showdown for power is coming and when it does come it will be a bloody battle.'

*

You bend your backs. You paddle hard. It's slow progress and bullets pop little spouts of water around your dinghy, like pebbles thrown by boys into a pond. This cold, dark, immense ocean is a pond now, a series of ponds.

You compose yourselves as the firing lessens. The bullets pop only from time to time. The spouts are fewer and fewer. You compose yourselves enough to take a compass bearing. You're pretty sure the submarine won't be there.

'She's not going to be there, no fucking way,' you say.

Bob says, 'Helpful, Tanky, helpful.'

You paddle on, but you're reaching further and further down to the water, the cold, dark, immense body of water beneath you is getting further and further away. Your paddles barely brush the surface.

'What the fuck?' Bob says.

Butch is shivering, saying nothing.

You lean over the side. And you see it. You see the emergency air bottle, the canister, has been knocked, and it's kicked in, and it's inflating the dinghy, it's still blowing it up.

'The bloody thing's still blowing up,' you shout.

But you start to laugh again. You're laughing as the dinghy gets fatter and fatter, and you're going slower and slower and any chance now of meeting the Safari *must be less than zero, surely.*

You're laughing, and you're not scared, you're not scared of death.

You don't wait for Bob to let you have it, so you lean over the side and you adjust the release valve. And the release valve wails, it lets out a high-pitched wail, which immediately gives away your position in the middle of this dark, cold, immense ocean that you're in.

And the enemy hears this wail and opens up again. Bullets skitter across the surface of the water, and you think of ducks and drakes, you think of ducks in a fairground shooting gallery, you think of ducks in a barrel.

And you think of Doris. You think of Doris 'cos you're not scared, you're not scared of death.

You bend your backs. You paddle hard.

The darkness is dense, pitch black, and you understand this phrase now. You think about North Africa, try to picture where it is, how long it would take to paddle back to Algiers.

Cheers, Algiers; Algiers, cheers, you think.

Sergeant Fitzpatrick is in the dinghy close by. The firing has stopped and Fitzpatrick is close by!

'How long it'd take, sarge?' you ask. 'How long you reckon, to paddle back, to paddle back to Algiers?'

Fitzpatrick replies. 'We'll make it.'
That's it, you realise:
That's *SAS* –
Confidence –
No task too big, no detail too small.

Storyteller

Harold 'Tanky' Challenor tells me two stories.

And only the one of them is true, he says.

The SAS boys are on training schemes in Algeria, trekking by a river. Tanky's carrying a bottle of beer, and he is very much looking forward to slaking his considerable thirst. But a bit of horseplay with one of the lads, and the bottle of beer ends up in the river. Tanky dives in to fetch it back. A crocodile clocks him and fancies some lunch. Harold 'Tanky' Challenor takes care of that crocodile with his army-issue knife and then climbs back out with the bottle held high like a trophy. And he very much enjoys his cold brown ale.

He's captured in Italy. SS interrogation: right old leathering. In the prisoner of war camp, he befriends a washerwoman. Using her nail file, he cuts through the barbed wire, escapes in her clothes, and walks miles south across Italy to rejoin his regiment.

Which one is true?

Does it even fucking matter?

Two

'That mad bastard Challenor!'

Challenor stalks the Mad House. He prowls the corridors. He's looking for Police Sergeant Alan Ratcliffe who, a few hours earlier, Challenor has heard, witnessed Wilf Gardiner threaten Johnnie Ford with a hammer. On top of this, on the way to West End Central, Wilf Gardiner informed Police Sergeant Alan Ratcliffe that he – Wilf Gardiner – is currently assisting Detective Sergeant Harold Challenor with an investigation into protection rackets in Soho run by Johnnie Ford and Riccardo Pedrini and, by association, Joseph 'King' Oliva.

Challenor's steaming, steaming along the corridors of West End Central, the Mad House.

He's not happy.

Where the fuck are you, Alan?

Challenor means business. He doesn't mess about, Challenor.

The corridors are empty. The word has got out that Challenor's not happy, and he suspects that these two facts are not unrelated.

Where the fuck are you, Alan?

Police Sergeant Alan Ratcliffe is not in the office. He's not in the locker room. He's not in the canteen. He's not in the cells. He's not in any of the interview rooms. And he is certainly not in the corridors.

Where the fuck *are you, Alan?*

Challenor has also heard that on the way to West End Central, Wilf Gardiner remarked to Johnnie Ford that when they got there, arrived at West End Central, he – Wilf Gardiner – was going to finger the lot of them, and that 'them' was understood to mean Johnnie Ford, Riccardo Pedrini and Joseph 'King' Oliva.

Challenor has also heard that on the way to West End Central, Johnnie Ford has remarked to Wilf Gardiner that he knows exactly what will happen to him if he is indeed to finger the lot of them. Ford added, Challenor has heard, that Wilf Gardiner's woman will not want to be seen with Wilf again after what they will do to him, should he indeed finger the lot of them.

Where the fuck *are you, Alan?*

Challenor knows Gardiner's woman: Elizabeth Ewing Evans. He's heard that she was there and witnessed this conversation.

He can't find her either.

Where the fuck are you, Alan?

*

You're silent, your back is bent, you're paddling hard. You're silent, all of you, to save your breath. It's a long paddle back to North Africa, after all.

Your paddles bite deep into the water. Your breaths are heavy with effort.

And then –

A beautiful sight –

The HMS Safari *looms like a surfaced whale.*

It's called a Nelson's blind eye when you ignore orders, in the Navy, when you know you're doing the right thing.

And the enemy must have known there was a bigger ship out there, you can't have paddled from North Africa, so there was considerable risk involved, you realise.

Good lads, the Navy. Staunch.

They hand round shots of Nelson's blood, a mud-thick, dark Pusser's rum, and you nail yours, and get hold of another.

'You lot stuck around for us gormless pongos?' you ask one of the sailors. 'Why were you silly bastards waiting for us?'

The sailor grins. 'We were halfway ready to come and help,' he says. 'The skipper was putting together a landing party. Lucky you, eh?'

Good lads, the Navy. Staunch.

You get hold of a tot more Nelson's blood and nail it.

Cheers, Algiers; Algiers, cheers.

*

Challoner's steaming, the radio's on in his office, where he is pacing the tiny room. The news –

News he listens to with agitated interest –

News of his old stomping ground, Algiers –

In Algiers, he hears, Colonel Hassan has seized control. This is only, how long, he thinks, two, three weeks since independence?

He's steaming, but he raises an eyebrow to his old stomping ground:

Cheers, Algiers; Algiers, cheers.

The radio moves on from the news and old Neil Sedaka's singing about breaking up being hard to do.

Challenor doesn't fancy Neil Sedaka much.

Where the fuck are you, Alan?

Where –

Radio's moved on from old Neil Sedaka. Challenor sighs a sigh of relief at that. A moment of respite. A, you know, what's the, what's the word, a *lull*. He's bent right out of shape, is Challenor, and he needs this lull, this respite, he thinks.

Radio news is back on: Oswald Mosley's been hammered at a

rally in Manchester. His right-wing mob's been proper turned over by the sound of it, and old Oswald's taken something of a personal leathering.

Good, thinks Challenor. Good –

Worthless Nazi cunt –

Good.

Challenor would likely have a go himself, he thinks, if he ever came across Mr Mosley.

We weren't hammering the krauts for the fun of it, he considers. *What are you going to do about it?*

And old Oswald's Nazi sympathiser chat is also bang out of order with respect to the German boys Challenor locked horns with. Not the SS – oh no sir, not those nasty little fuckers – but the infantry, the *lads*, the lads Challenor, yes – the lads Challenor locked horns with.

What are you going to do about it?

What are you *going to do about it?*

So –

Yes, very good news indeed.

Still –

Where the fuck are you, Alan?

Where –

'Detective Sergeant Challenor,' says Police Sergeant Alan Ratcliffe, his head poking around the door to Challenor's office. 'A word?'

'Alan,' Challenor says. 'It'll be more than one word, I hope.' Challenor gestures for him to sit down. 'Sit down, Alan,' he says.

'Cheeseman,' says Ratcliffe.

'That's only one word, Alan.'

Ratcliffe smiles. 'Well, you know the others.'

'I think I likely do.' Challenor smiles back. 'Alan John Cheeseman, *Alan*, I believe is who you're talking about. Why don't you – why don't you fill me in on it all, either way, eh, Alan?'

'Short version?'

'No detail too small, Alan.'

Police Sergeant Alan Ratcliffe shifts in his seat. 'We've been keeping an eye, as you are well aware, on the Phoenix and Geisha clubs, at your request of course, knowing that something of a feud is developing between Wilf Gardiner and Johnnie Ford's boys.'

'Yes, Alan.'

'Earlier this evening, one of our PCs – PC Laing – spotted Ford, King, Pedrini and Alan John Cheeseman gather at the Lyric pub on Great Windmill Street. You know it?'

'Yes, Alan.'

'The lads seemed tense, according to PC Laing, and he decided to hang back and see what might be going on. Sensible lad, PC Laing.'

'Yes, Alan.'

'PC Laing calls me and I decide to set up a watch with immediate effect at both the Phoenix and Geisha clubs.'

Ratcliffe pulls a packet of cigarettes from his shirt pocket and gestures with it. 'Do you mind, guv?'

'No, Alan.'

Ratcliffe takes a long drag from his cigarette and exhales, slowly. 'So outside the Phoenix club we see Wilf Gardiner's car. You know it? Very nice motor, distinctive, hard to miss.'

'Yes, Alan.'

'And Wilf Gardiner is standing next to his car, on the pavement side, right by the entrance to the Phoenix club. And his missus – Elizabeth Ewing Evans – is standing next to him. You know her?'

'Yes, Alan.'

'And they seem in reasonable spirits, and Gardiner's spotted me, and he's waved, and, like I say, they seem in reasonable spirits.'

Challenor's breathing heavy. He feels his shoulders roll and tense. He snorts. He's like a bull, they say, when he's not happy.

He knows they say this, and he knows that Police Sergeant Alan Ratcliffe knows they say this, and yet he is not getting very quickly to the point.

'Point, Alan, please.'

Ratcliffe nods and shifts once again in his seat. 'After a short time, PC Laing tails Ford, King, Pedrini and Cheeseman from Great Windmill Street, down Berwick, then we watch as they approach the Phoenix club, from Old Compton.'

Challenor sits stiller. His breathing steadies. He's not afraid, he's never afraid, never afraid once it's all begun, once it's kicked off, once the game has really started. And now that Ratcliffe is getting to the point, he feels like it *has* all begun, and he knows this and a calm – a degree of calm – settles over him.

'Cheeseman is another one from the manor, it turns out. Unemployed salesman, twenty years old, lives at home with his parents, good mates with Pedrini, helps out at the Pedrini family restaurant from time to time.'

Challenor's breathing intensifies.

'Point, Alan, *please.*'

'So they approach the Phoenix club from Old Compton and Gardiner's clocked them and he's turned to me and yelled "these are the slags!" and the same time, he's hustled Elizabeth Ewing Evans to one side, and he's reached into his car and pulled out a hammer.'

'A hammer, Alan?'

'Yes, a hammer.'

'And what did Gardiner do with this hammer?'

Police Sergeant Alan Ratcliffe nods and shifts once again in his seat. He folds his cigarette into the ashtray that Challenor keeps on his desk.

'Not a lot, in the end. There was a good deal of shouting. Gardiner seemed especially keen to get at Ford. More shouting.

Something about a tart that works for Gardiner. Seems Johnnie Ford may not be as gallant a chap as we first thought, Detective Challenor.'

'I never once thought that, Alan.'

'Well, you know what I mean. These young Italian stallions, is what I mean.'

'Yes, Alan.'

'So we break it up and we restrain Gardiner and his hammer, and Pedrini's telling us to book Gardiner for threatening them with an offensive weapon, and we've seen him do it, so it's tricky.'

'What did Gardiner say at this point, Alan?'

'Gardiner said he was using the hammer to knock a dent out of his car, and to be fair, his car was in a bit of a state.'

Challenor smiles. 'I know all about Wilf Gardiner's car, Alan.'

'And this is where things got a little confused.'

'Yes, Alan.'

Challenor leans forward.

'We bring Gardiner to West End Central, on foot, and Ford and Pedrini and King and Cheeseman follow to make voluntary statements regarding Wilf Gardiner's use of an offensive weapon.'

'I'll stop you here, Alan,' Challenor says, 'to speed things up. I believe this is when the discussion between Gardiner and Ford concerning Gardiner being a grass and assisting me with my enquiries took place. Is this right?'

'Yes, guv.'

'Good, Alan. Now. I understand that none of these unsavoury characters remain here at West End Central, despite you bringing all of them in.'

'Well, we brought Gardiner *in*, the others – '

'Alan?'

Police Sergeant Alan Ratcliffe looks down. 'On the way to West End Central, on hearing Gardiner explain that he was assisting you, and after an unpleasant verbal exchange, Ford, Pedrini, King and Cheeseman took flight.'

'And what was the exact nature of this verbal exchange, Alan?'

Police Sergeant Alan Ratcliffe looks forlorn. 'Well, Pedrini, on hearing that you and Gardiner were perhaps in cahoots in some way – his words – made it very plain that he would not be joining the rest of them at West End Central to press this offensive weapon charge. And Pedrini persuaded the others to leave with him.'

'And what was the exact nature of Pedrini's complaint, Alan?'

Police Sergeant Alan Ratcliffe looks uncertain. 'Pedrini, well, Pedrini seemed, he, um, Pedrini thought, well, he said, more or less this: "No chance I'm having anything to with that Challenor. I bet he hates Italians. I'm not taking a slap from him. He'll stitch us up."'

'Hates Italians? Those were his words, his exact words?'

Police Sergeant Alan Ratcliffe nods.

'Hates Italians, eh?' Challenor says, nodding, brow furrowed. 'You can go now, Alan,' he says. 'We'll talk tomorrow. Next steps, next moves. Well done, my old son. You did all right there, tonight, you did.'

Police Sergeant Alan Ratcliffe nods and leaves.

Hates Italians, eh? Challenor thinks. That's something, that is. That really is something.

*

Italy, 7 September 1943: Operation Speedwell.

Finally.

You've been playing at soldiers for a few months after the Sardinia debacle.

Debacle –

Well, your only regret is that you didn't get to kill any of the enemy –

You faced them, faced their fire, and felt no fear.

Passed the test you'd set yourself. A test you didn't even know you'd set yourself, but once you'd passed it you knew –

You've been recovering from a bout of malaria. The mosquitoes in Philippeville in Algeria are monsters. The buggers had you for break- fast, lunch, dinner. You never took your pills – you thought you could beat the disease, beat the buggers – the monsters *– by force of will, by* sheer *character.*

Ten days in a military hospital, shivering, you were.

They tell you you'll never really ever get rid of it, that there's after- effects, too, sometimes, so to be careful.

What after-effects exactly, they don't tell you.

It bent you right out, did the bout of malaria. But you beat it down, for now, you beat it down.

And now, Italy. Operation Speedwell.

You're going to be dropped behind the lines. Which means a bit of the old cloak and dagger. You smoke, so they give you a pipe with a tiny compass in the stem; a silk map of Italy stitched into the tobacco pouch. It means you are learning a bit of Italian, and you're good at it.

And of course, it means parachute training –

Of course it fucking does: Special Air Service.

Not that it bothers you, oh no –

A man who has no fear has nothing to conquer.

The training jumps are exhilarating, the slipstream growl, the blind step out, the incredible rushing noise as the chute opens, the pull of the harness, and then you float there, on air, you float on air, and you don't even feel it as you hit the earth and roll forward just as you've been shown, down here, down here on the ground.

Yes, exhilarating.

And you're itching to do it for real, you are.

Operation Speedwell, or what you call: The Italian job.

*

Challenor's working on the next steps, the next moves, quicker than he might have anticipated.

He's got Police Constable David Harris in his office. Harris is telling Challenor about an incident he witnessed not two hours ago. He is a confident young man, Challenor thinks, a good bearing to him. He likes the cut of Police Constable David Harris's jib, Challenor does. And this means he is likely to listen more calmly, question a little less aggressively, be more inclined to trust him, and this is pleasing.

'So, David, tell me.'

'Well, guv, I was posted outside the Phoenix as per. Was a quiet night for them, I felt, on the whole, you know, in general. Not a lot of business, I'd say, you know, relatively.'

'Yes, David.'

'I gave myself a few minutes to go for a bite, just to pick up a sandwich, you know, as per, and when I came back they were there.'

'Who were there, David?'

'Ford and Pedrini and Gardiner.'

'This does not come as a considerable surprise, David, and I suspect that it is not a surprise to you.'

'It is not, guv, no.'

'No, David, I should think it isn't. And what happened next?'

'Well, guv, Gardiner was looking rather white, I'd say, his back was against the wall and he was white, even, I'd say, a little green round the gills, if you know what I mean?'

'I do know what you mean, David.'

'And Ford and Pedrini were, I'd say, threatening him, or at least speaking in no uncertain terms, though about what exactly I won't speculate.'

'Please do speculate, David.'

'Well, guv, they appeared to be having a disagreement regarding a girl that works at Gardiner's club.'

'That's all, would you say, *speculating*, I mean?'

'A sum of money was discussed. A hundred pounds.'

'In what context, David?'

'Oh, in the "you're going to give us a hundred pounds or what are you going to do" context, guv.'

Challenor nods. 'Speculating suits you, David, I think. And you intervened, I assume?'

'I did, guv. There was no evidence of an actual crime, but I took down the particulars of the two men. Pedrini gave his real name. Ford called himself "Williams".'

'And you didn't pull him up on this falsehood, knowing, as you do, that Ford is called Ford.'

'I did not, guv.'

Challenor nods and smiles. 'Excellent decision, David. You can go now.'

Police Constable David Harris nods and leaves.

Challenor thinks he could use this young lad.

*

The Italian job –

Goal: to blow up trains in the tunnels of the Apennines, a long, long way behind the lines.

This is the easy part, you think. The hard part? Getting back to friendly faces. By guess or by God, you reckon.

And the jump, oh the jump, you think. Fair enough, you like a jump, you're good at it, it's easy for you, it doesn't scare you, but you've not done one at night, and the dropping zone is unprepared. Unprepared? You haven't got a fucking clue what you're going to find down there. You're relying on Shank's pony and a hard slog.

But you get it, you see why, and you see you're going to make a difference, big picture-wise, one way or another.

You're assigned the line between La Spezia and Bologna.

'Sounds tasty,' you say, smacking your lips, to Lieutenant Wedderburn, your mission companion, your senior. He smiles. He's a posh Scot, old Wedderburn, and you're happy enough with him.

He's 'Sir'; you're 'Tanky'. That's that.

End of.

*

Challenor's got Police Constable Patrick Goss in his office. Police Constable Patrick Goss has some news regarding the next steps, the next moves.

He's telling Challenor about what he witnessed earlier that evening by Piccadilly Circus.

Radio's playing 'The Loco-motion' by Little Eva. Challenor likes this one, likes Little Eva, likes Little Eva's voice, her style, is glad that she's top of the hit parade.

Loco-motion: mad moves.

All that chug-a motion, that railroad train, makes Challenor think of Italy, of Speedwell, of the Italian job.

He smiles.

Goss says, 'Gardiner was in his car with his mistress, Elizabeth Ewing Evans, when a van pulled up, a van driven by Joseph Francis Oliva and with James Thomas Fraser in the passenger seat, and Jean Murray – Oliva's bird – in the back.'

Challenor's listening, but he knows where this is going and he's fed up with sitting in his office listening to Police Constable Patrick Goss tell him things he already knows. And besides, with Little Eva on, his mind wanders, drifts over to the Yanks, and that poor slag

Monroe who carked it only a few days ago. Silly tart, filling herself up with pills and booze.

If it was her that did it, of course. Challenor's of a mind to think the unfortunate girl may well have been *offed*.

'…and Fraser shouts "are you still grassing?" and then appears to lash out with something, something metallic, there was definitely a sort of flash…'

Challenor knows this is important stuff that Goss is telling him. He recognises that this young lad's testimony, his incident report, ties together Ford and Pedrini most definitively with Joseph 'King' Oliva. This is a very useful connection.

'…and when I stop the van a little way down the road, the two of them tell me that Gardiner was driving recklessly, trying to get them into a sort of Yank drag race, and there's no sign of any metallic object…'

Challenor knows it's about time he gets out there and has a word with this lot and starts nicking them. He doesn't need much and there will always be a way to make something stick with these disreputable young men. Uncle Harry will bring them in, no time. And Brass want them inside, after all, off the streets.

'…so I let them go and then talk to Gardiner who claims they were waving a bayonet at him, a fucking *bayonet*, sorry, sir, and this Evans sort tells me that Fraser added "when we do up your old man, we'll do you up too", so she's a little shaken, understandably…'

Nice and easy, son. Don't lose control.

Challenor rocks gently along to Little Eva's swing, her rhythm.

'…and Gardiner's mentioned you, sir, and told me to report all this and to say that he's getting it in the neck almost daily from this mob, and all you've got to do is be out and you'll see it, and Bob's your uncle…'

'He said what, Patrick?'

'He said, that all you've got to do – '

'Oh, I heard, Patrick. I just wanted to be clear that Mr Gardiner is telling me – through you – telling *me* what to do. Would you say that's a fair assessment, Patrick?'

Nice and easy, son. Don't lose control.

'I would, sir, yes.'

Nice and easy, son. Don't lose control.

'Thank you, Patrick. You can go now.'

*

Night.

Sky a deep blue-black. Cloudless. The clank and whirr of the plane's engines a skittering, low thrum. A growl.

You're growling, crawling through the deep blue-black night sky, growling, crawling your way from Africa to Italy.

Italy. Italy –

Italy, where you're going to blow up trains with Lieutenant Wedderburn, on the line that runs from Bologna to La Spezia. Italy. You don't know much of the language at all, but you're learning, haven't a clue about the old, the old – what's the word? – the old local customs. You're worried that there is a fairly high chance that you're going to stick out like a shiny sixpence on a sweep's backside.

Pitch black on the plane as you approach the lines. Cramped, too. And no smoking, blackout respect is total, no orange glows, no tasty little respite to be had from the skitter and whirr bringing you closer to Italy –

Italy.

Nothing to do but doze or chat. You chat. Course you do. A lively debate on the respective merits of Italian and Arab women, of Italian and Arab booze. Lively, yes, but ignorant, you know that, no one has a bloody clue. You all decide that, yes, where you're headed, there are very likely to be better versions of both.

The engines though are loud, their skitter and clank ratcheted up as your altitude shifts up and down, better to avoid any inconvenient local traffic. So there are long periods of silence.

You're all likely thinking the same thing –

What are we going to find when we get down there?

Or, more, more – what's the word? – you know, more pertinent –

What is going to find you?

What the fuck is going to find you, you think, you're thinking now, you're thinking what the fuck is going to find you, you know, when you get down there?

Down to Italy.

You stare at your fellow men. In the darkness, in the deep darkness of the deep blue-black sky, and with your faces blackened, you can only see their white teeth. Their yellowing teeth, their nicotine-stained yellowing teeth that in this darkness are white.

Movement at the front of the plane. Radio-crackle. Signalling from the co-pilot to your seniors, your officers. Green-light. Hatch opens and your sweat immediately cools as the slipstream pours in, roars in. Unbuckle, strap in. Check the static lines, check the equipment, check each other's equipment, check the ties on each other's chutes, in the dim light that is switched on.

Get into jumping order.

Captain Dudgeon speaks: 'Watch your drift going down. The stick is to stay as tight as possible. I will remain where I land and you are to walk to me, number six walking on to number five and so on until we pick each other up.'

You're not listening. You're not listening as you're thinking about what the fuck is going to find you, *you're not listening as you know all this, it's been drilled into you and you're ready, you're all ready and you're not afraid, but you'd love a smoke, a moment to steel yourself, but you won't get it.*

You check the time. Three o'clock kick-off. You smile at that.

———

Green-light flash –
'Number One!'
And Dudgeon vanishes into the night, vanishes into the deep blue-black night.

*

Challenor's had enough of the office, had enough sitting, sitting around, talking, talking to police constables, so he's outside, he's outside in Soho, outside on his streets in Soho, *doing –*

What are you going to do *about it?*

Police Constable David Harris has been keeping an eye on a number of establishments each evening over the past few weeks. These establishments include the pubs: the Lyric on Great Windmill Street, the Three Greyhounds on the corner of Moor Street and Old Compton, the Spice of Life at the end of Moor and interestingly located opposite Wilf Gardiner's Geisha club. Police Constable David Harris has also been keeping an eye on the 2i's coffee bar on Old Compton, the Colony Room on Dean Street, and Trisha's after-hours spot on Greek. Challenor suspects that Police Constable David Harris has earmarked these latter three establishments for reasons not entirely pertaining to their investigation. Challenor has heard that young Harris is something of what Challenor believes is termed a 'scenester' and has earmarked these particular establishments for his own advancement within the particular 'scene' that Challenor has heard young Harris enjoys.

Challenor has walked past the 2i's coffee bar a large number of times and its popularity never ceases to amaze. Yank music live in the basement is what does it, he thinks. Young men posing with their greased hair and their style boots and their style jackets, combing this greased hair of theirs, smoking their fags while combing this greased-back hair that they have. And girls, screaming. Wetting their knickers, if old Wilf Gardiner knows what he's about, these girls are, wetting them, they are, *soaking* them, so Wilf Gardiner says. Challenor's contempt for Wilf Gardiner is increasing by the day.

Challenor's not sure about this scene. He's a Motown man, likes the darkie soul music, does Challenor. And why not? He wants to feel less – not more – hysterical. And the Motown singers – especially the women Motown singers – they do that to him, with their rhythm and their groove, and their voices and their style.

But Challenor's not going to any of these establishments. Challenor does not mess about.

What are you going to do about it?

Challenor's headed to the Coffee Pot on Brewer Street because that's where he's going to find five men he believes are at the heart of this protection racket that is threatening old Wilf Gardiner almost daily, and Uncle Harry has it in mind to have a word, and scope these ne'er do wells first hand.

*

You're Number Six.

And the green-light flash, and then you're gasping in the icy slipstream, and your stomach drops as you free fall for seconds that feel like long, long hours, and then you're jerked up and up by your shoulders and you check your rigging lines are clear, not tangled, and you see the plane disappear to your right, and you look ahead and there is the rest of the stick, swaying gently in a straight, perfect formation, and you think of skiing in Scotland and jumping in Egypt where you trained, and the deep blue-black night is still, and you reckon you could have a nice chat in this deep blue-black, still, cool, cool night –

Seven thousand feet up in the air and sound doesn't half travel.

So you keep your traps shut.

Seven thousand feet up in the air and it isn't half cold.

But it is cloudless and moonlit and the Apennines look like England's green and pleasant, they do, to you, from up there, from seven thousand feet up in the air.

Where everything floats, floats for a while, evaporates, cools –

For a little while, you don't worry too much about what the fuck is going to find you down there. In Italy –

Italy.

*

'Lads.'

Heads turn.

'Fuck do you want?' says Pedrini to Challenor.

Challenor pulls up a chair. 'That's no way to talk to your Uncle Harry, young man.' Challenor helps himself to a mug of tea from the pot on the table. 'Your old mum didn't teach you any manners?'

Challenor slurps his tea. He examines the interior of the Coffee Pot on Brewer Street and thinks he understands why Police Constable David Harris isn't so wild about this place, lacking, as it does, much style, much *glamour*.

'Biscuit, Uncle Harry?' says Ford. 'You know, to go with your tea?'

There are guffaws. Challenor grins. 'I couldn't trouble you for a chocolate bourbon, I suppose?' His grin widens, his eyes narrow. 'We didn't get many of them in the war, you know, behind the lines, in, you know, France, *Italy*.'

Silence.

'You been there then, Harry?' says Pedrini.

Challenor gives him the fisheye. There's Pedrini, Ford, Cheeseman and Oliva – these Challenor was expecting. There's another lad, too, that Challenor recognises: Fraser. Goes by the alias Fraser the Razor, he's heard, Challenor has. That's five. There's one missing, Challenor thinks, if Harris has been doing his job right. He wonders who it might be.

'I spent some time there, yes, young man,' Challenor says, still grinning. 'You know what we did? During the war?'

Challenor stands. He continues, 'They dropped me behind the lines with nothing but a pistol and a knife and a bag of dynamite and told me to blow up your Italian trains.'

He places his palms on the table, leans over the lads. He says, 'We did it, too. That bit was easy. Made friends with some of the locals. Got quite close to one of them, if you know what I mean.'

Challenor sits back down. The five lads are all smoking and examining each other, and examining the walls, examining anything, in fact, that keeps them out of Challenor's eye line.

Silence.

Challenor settles himself back into his chair. He's throne-ing this hard-backed, wooden chair, in this faintly grotty, very basic caff, which seems to have been picked by this gang of five solely for its lack of attraction for many others. There were three other customers when Challenor walked in. Now there are none. The proprietor is drying something with a tea towel, though Challenor has noticed that he's been drying something with a tea towel for quite some time. Challenor's not sure if the proprietor's somewhat hostile look refers to him, or to the five lads with whom he is attempting to converse, with whom he is attempting to *have a word*.

The lights are on low for your basic caff, Challenor thinks, and there are assorted framed pictures and photographs and posters on the walls, but Challenor identifies no obvious theme to this collection.

The lads are dressed in a uniform of sorts – black suits, white shirts, black ties, carefully sculpted hair, *crafted* hair, really, close cropped, but not *too* close, just long enough to allow a little sculpting, a little *crafting*.

'What did you do in the war then, lads?' Challenor asks.

The lads smoke. The lads shuffle in their seats. They shuffle in their seats, Challenor thinks, less than comfortably.

Ford says, 'The war? We were busy being born, Uncle Harry.'

There is laughter. There is nervous laughter.

'Oh,' says Challenor, 'so it was your good mothers who were busy in the war then, busy, doing things, *service*, if you like, back then, in the war.' He pauses and grins, wider still. 'Good for them. Good for your old mums.'

Silence.

Five lads seethe –

Challenor eyes Oliva.

*

The first thing that finds you down there, in Italy, down there on the ground in Italy, is a fucking tree.

But, you know what, thank fuck for this Italian tree. It doesn't half break your fall. Fortunately, it's your canopy-type, umbrella sort of a tree, with its soft enough branches and its abundant leaves and, you know what, you slip quite nicely through it, you do, and land like a cat that's pirouetted off a kitchen counter down to his little bowl of milk, all happy and smooth like.

Seven thousand feet, and you end up falling about a half dozen, really only that, it feels, to land, softly, in Italy, down there, on the ground in Italy.

First thing, you think: parachute. Before anything else: parachute. And while your Italian tree was a definite ally in aiding the smoothness and comfort of your landing, it's a fucking pain in the, you know, it is now, right now, it's a fucking right pain in the backside.

Rigging's caught across about ten feet of branches, so first thing, first thing, is you shin up the tree, shin up the way you've just come down, and cut the rigging out of the tree with your army-issue knife. And your army-issue knife might be quite the thing to stick into the gut of a German sentry, but its serrated edge is not, you're realising, quite the sharpest tool in the box. Quite a fucking effort, it is, shinning up to where you've just come down from, cutting out the bloody rigging, with a bloody blunt army-issue blade. You're basically having to saw through the rigging with this blunt blade, and you're cursing its thickness, until you remember the bloody rigging kept you up in the air not long ago and you were pretty bloody thankful for the thickness of the bloody rigging, not that long ago. And this tickles you, this really tickles you, the relief, you suppose, the relief of it all, and you laugh, quite loud, and quite long, until you remember where you are, and why, and quite how still the cool, cool night is, down here, in Italy, and you shut your fucking trap, sharpish.

*

But Oliva ain't biting.

No, *signori*, Oliva ain't biting. He's sat, looking bored, staring at the collection of photographs and posters and pictures on the walls, studying them, he is, but not with any conviction, any gusto, any *bottle*.

What are you going to do about it?

'What say you, young Joseph?' Challenor asks. 'You're awfully quiet, young man, I must say, for, you know, the *leader*.' Challenor grins. 'That noble, no, *scusa ragazzo*, that… *regal* bearing you have doesn't quite match up with this shy and retiring, this wallflower act.'

Oliva turns, slowly.

Challenor notes this slow turn and sees in it a measure of confidence. Challenor notes this confidence. He's not sure what to do with it, this confidence, just yet.

Oliva says, 'You've got some face, *Uncle Harry*, coming in here. Some serious face, you've got. I'll give you that, your face.'

Oliva shoots a look –

Oliva stands, pushes his wooden chair back, gives the empty room a final once over, looks across the room with its collection of posters and pictures and photographs, nods at the proprietor, subtle, but a definite inclination of the bonce, and leaves.

After Oliva leaves, Ford, Pedrini, Cheeseman, Fraser and King leave.

Challenor grins –

We're on, son, he thinks. We're only fucking on.

*

The rigging gives in the end, after a half hour or so of fannying about with your less than effective army-issue knife, sawing at the ropes, first one way then t'other –

And down it comes, in a tangled heap on the ground –

Which, at this point, isn't a great deal better than stuck up a tree.

You bend your back and dig a nice little grave for your trusty chute, your thick, sturdy chute, and it turns out that your army-issue knife is rather better equipped for this, and you've buried your chute, and given it a little lay-to-rest, R.I.P salute, and you're on your way in about a quarter hour.

You use your watch and the stars –

You're looking for Wedderburn, who is looking for Foster, who is looking for Shortall, who is looking for Pinckney, who is looking for Greville-Bell, who is looking for Dudgeon.

Low whistling is the pre-arranged signal. You know the line along which the five in front of you in the stick should *have landed. But you ended up arse-clamped in a tree, so what do* you *know?*

What are you going to do about it?

You whistle and you move, you move and you whistle –
You whistle and you move along the axis where your compadres
should, you know, more or less, be.
Italy. Italy –
Cheers, Algiers; Algiers, cheers.

*

Challenor's at Wilf Gardiner's other place, the Phoenix. Fortunately, Wilf Gardiner's at the Geisha, so Challenor doesn't have to listen to his bunny, his *pony*, and can simply get on with his job –

What are you going to do about it, eh?

'So,' Challenor says, to Elizabeth Ewing Evans, Wilf Gardiner's, for want of a better one, mistress, 'give me your humble in terms of this sorry little saga.'

Elizabeth Ewing Evans is smoking. She takes a long drag on a long fag, one of those thin ones, black with gold tips, a foreign name, Sobranie, he thinks, a very *ladylike* cigarette, this one, all told. She says, 'I wouldn't call it a saga, detective.' She smiles. The gold tip of her very ladylike cigarette is bruised purple-red from her lipstick. 'Saga suggests something epic, which suggests heroism, which suggests valour, which, in turn, suggests *value*, which, of course, suggests this sorry little saga has been worthwhile.'

'I think – '

'I'm aware, detective, of the irony in your question. "Sorry little saga", yes, got it.' Evans smiles again.

Challenor nods. 'Irony or otherwise, I'm still interested in your thoughts.' He pauses. 'Beyond, I mean, your overall *sense* of the thing. That much I can gather, of course, from your irony.'

Elizabeth Ewing Evans folds her thin, black, gold-tipped, foreign cigarette into the ashtray in front of her.

It's fairly quiet, the Phoenix, for this time, on a Thursday. A half-dozen suited types, tourists, Challenor thinks, to look at them, down from places like Rochdale, and Stockport, and Huddersfield, Challenor reckons, by their brogues, by their radiating Northernness. Down for a conference or other, Challenor suspects, and living it up in old Soho, with a few jars and a few dances, what with the missus tucked away with the kids up there in Rochdale, and Stockport, and Huddersfield.

The dancers, Challenor sees, are doing very well for themselves, on autopilot they are –

Candy-from-a-baby situation.

Not your calibre of bird, of dancer, Challenor listens in to the Northerners' discussion, not the same *quality*, back home, they say. Bright lights and whatnot. Carpe Diem and Bob's your fooking uncle, and more money finds its way into the pockets, the straps really, of this better calibre of bird, of dancer, that you've got down here, down here in glamorous Soho.

'It's all a bit handbags in the playground, I'd say, Detective Challenor.'

'Oh yes?'

'That's certainly how it started, at least.'

'And how did it start?'

Elizabeth Ewing Evans plucks and slides another thin, black, foreign cigarette from the shiny, silver cigarette case that's on the table. With a flick of her wrist she both lights the cigarette and summons a waitress. Well, a waitress appears, though, to be fair, Challenor's not sure the two things – the flick of the wrist; the appearance of the waitress – are necessarily part of a causal relationship.

'Another?' the waitress asks Challenor.

Challenor turns his bottle of brown ale. The Phoenix is, like the Geisha, after all, famous for its brown ale –

Challenor considers this and nods. 'Go on then,' he says, and, looking at Elizabeth Ewing Evans, he adds, 'in for a penny, eh?'

'It's Wilf's old friend Fat Juan that's provoked all this.' Ms Evans exhales for a long time. Your foreign, sophisticated fag will do that, Challenor thinks. 'You can trace the origin of all this to a night a few months ago,' she adds.

'Not long after Fat Juan got out then.'

'Not long at all. And it's pertinent, I'd say. You know what they say about Juan, of course…'

Challenor nods.

'…well he was in here, not long after he got out, bear that in mind, and what it means, like I say, pertinent, *you* know what I mean.'

'I do know what you mean.'

'And, well, let's just say that this is unsurprising, when he was in here, he took something of a shine to one of our dancers.'

Challenor's head bobs. He says, 'Knowing Fat Juan, by reputation at least, this does not come as a considerable surprise, no.'

Elizabeth Ewing Evans nods. 'Thing is, the dancer, one of our younger ladies, something else I suspect you won't find a considerable surprise, is called Maria. Maria. So, you know.'

'Aha,' Challenor says. 'I believe I do know.'

'Quite.'

'Cousin or something? Sister? Or lover situation?' Challenor says. 'They tend not to be the most accommodating in either scenario, I've always found, your Italian family.'

Elizabeth Ewing Evans nods again. 'Our young Maria,' she says, 'is a cousin of Riccardo Pedrini, and has been seen, from time to time, about town on the arm of a certain Joseph Oliva.'

'Well, I never,' Challenor says.

'Your turn to be ironic, I suppose.'

Challenor grins.

Elizabeth Ewing Evans continues. 'And an interesting little aside to this, is that the clan Pedrini had no idea that their butter-wouldn't-melt youngest cousin was plying a trade at Wilf Gardiner's Phoenix cabaret and revue bar.'

'To give it its full name.'

'To give it its full name, yes, tax purposes and so on.'

Challenor's head bobs again. 'So what, Fat Juan gets fruity, and young Maria doesn't like it, says see you *più tardi, amico…*'

Ms Elizabeth Ewing Evans raises her eyebrows to a fairly astonishing height at this spot of tongue, Challenor notes.

'…but old Fat Juan doesn't like this,' Challenor goes on, 'turns on his charm, gets tossed by your gorillas, cursing the little *puta*, and young Maria thinks maybe it's time her boyfriend and cousin get involved.'

'You're spot on, detective. He was just oil on the fire, Juanito, in the end. The clan Pedrini are after my Wilf, and so you're up to speed.'

'Bigger fish.'

'Bigger fish, that's right. Last time I saw the young Italians, they shouted after me, "We're going to stripe that bastard fella of yours."' She draws long on her foreign fag, her long, thin, foreign fag. 'I'd always thought Italians were cut from a more sophisticated linen.'

'So it's personal under the guise of a protection scam then?'

'Or the other way round, yes.'

Challenor nods –

His head bobs.

'I don't know why a nice young lady like you is having anything to do with these two-bob punters,' he says.

'One of them born every minute.'

Either way, he thinks.

'So long, sweetheart,' Challenor says. 'Be lucky.'

*

You whistle and you move, you move and you whistle. You've landed on a hillside, you've landed on a hillside in a copse, in a copse surrounded by shrub, by bush, by the deep blue-black, cool, cool night –

Silence.

And then you hear it, like an owl, an almost hoot, a not-quite owlish hoot, this low whistle that you hear. And you keep on the bearing to where you believe Wedderburn should be, and this low whistle seems to be on the line that you're walking, at least you suspect it is –

Silence –

Then again.

You form the sound with words in your head:

Whit Whooooo

This tickles you. You laugh to yourself. And it's infectious, this laughter. And you laugh harder. Here you are, in Italy, alone, behind enemy lines, deep behind enemy lines, sure to be executed on the spot, on sight, if stumbled upon by the wrong fella, and you're giggling –

Inside, you're giggling, you're tickled and you're laughing as you try to form the sound of this low whistle in words, or something like them, in your head –

Whit Whooooo

Silence –

You move and you whistle.

*

Challenor thinks he'll stop by the Geisha club, see old Wilf, seeing as Elizabeth Ewing Evans has given such considerable insight, such food for – you know, you know the word – thought. Quite an appraisal she's given him, Challenor thinks, and it strikes him, it strikes Challenor now, that the iron is hot. He reckons he might get a little more out of old Wilf now he knows the actual, genuine origin of this sorry little saga –

About time he felt some collars. He needs to sus these lads, get them inside.

What he was brought in for, after all, by Brass, as he's been reminded often enough, to clean up this Soho sewer, by any means necessary, and, after all, enough *is* enough, isn't it?

Enough's a bloody nuff, Challenor reckons, and grins.

He keeps his head down on Old Compton Street, passes the Three Greyhounds, which is heaving, crammed with drinkers and smokers and cheer. Lamps lit low and stout and ale thick, and one or two spilling out onto the pavement and Challenor ducks his bonce further, dips his chin into his coat, and keeps his head down.

He's across the road and in through the velvet curtains of the Phoenix, skips the stairs two at a time, and he's in.

Radio's on. The Four Seasons singing about some bird Sherry. Frankie Valli giving it the high-pitched yearn, the wail. *Can you come out tonight?*

Challenor likes this one, its got welly, bit of soul, it swings, *sways*. Yeah, he's all right, old Frankie Valli.

Couple of punters give Challenor the sidelong fisheye. One or two visibly shrink, turn away. Couple of the dancers give the tiniest nod of acknowledgement. They know it's no bad thing if a copper as notorious as Challenor is in attendance. No one plays up, no one's going to take liberties, not with Uncle Harry in attendance.

What are you going to do about it?

Challenor adopts a business pose: thick neck forward, head tilted across, eyes narrowed, his bull-like frame tensed, not quite crouched, ready, if necessary, to spring into sudden and irrevocable violence.

It's the impression that counts –

'Brown ale,' Challenor says to a passing waitress. 'I'll take it at the bar.'

The waitress nods and scurries off, her outfit pure Weimar camp.

Challenor lurches to the bar, *muscles* to the bar, his thick frame squat and hard.

'I'll be wanting a word with your guvnor,' he tells the waitress when she delivers his brown ale and asks if he'd like anything else.

Off she scurries, again, in her kit. Challenor shakes his head at the back of her scurrying figure. It's no job this, dressed up like a foxy Fraulein, like a Bavarian bitch in heat, all the promise of a jug of industrial lager – and a wink to match its strength.

Challenor feels for her, his waitress –

But that's not why he's here, so he gives his head another shake, to clear it, to settle it, and he thinks about the proposal he is about to outline to old Wilf.

It's a cracker. It really is.

Two birds situation and no mistake –

Challenor grins.

*

There he is, you think, there's Wedderburn, and there's Foster, and there's Shortall, and there's Greville-Bell, and there's Pinckney, and there's Dudgeon.

You made it, you've found each other on this cool, cool, deep, dark night, and it seems the whole stick has gone smoother than your rosy red behind, smooth as silk, smoother than a wop cocksman, someone says, and you all laugh, quietly.

Next few hours you rest. You keep your mouths shut and you rest –

The chatter of the birds wakes you up –

They speak English then, someone says, and you laugh, quietly.

The red sun is fat and crawling up from behind the Apennines –

Italy. Beautiful Italy.

You shin up a tree – you're getting good at this – and, with your binoculars, you locate the containers carrying the kit, the equipment.

There they are, their red and blue chutes standing out on the hillside like the proverbial. You and three others recover them and the first thing to do after you've buried and given the last rites to the chutes is to brew up, open tins of bully, and get some army-issue fuel inside of you.

Then you're confirming your position by what's around you, and all bloody day it takes, all bloody day studying maps and compass bearings, checking against the landmarks all around you, shinning up and down trees, checking, checking, checking all day, all bloody day until nightfall, and the next move.

A rendezvous is set: seven nights from now, at a specific point, on a specific stream, at a specific distance between Pontremoli and Villafranca.

You split into your pairings, and scatter into the night –

Low-key goodbyes and good lucks.

Off they march, the others, down a wooded mountain track, in single file, these men you're here with, in Italy, behind the lines, deep behind the lines, these men, carrying explosives to blow up trains and make a significant dent in the German plans to advance.

There they go in the cool, fresh, Italian night, the mountain air invigorating –

Will you ever see them again?

A dog barks, far away, in a distant village –

A guard dog, no doubt. And you think, as you trudge behind Wedderburn –

With any luck, quite soon, I'll be killing my first Jerry sentry. You think, to yourself, quite clearly, 'With any luck, I'll soon be killing my first Jerry sentry.'

Tanky was round my grandad's place once, I'd say early 80s, and
there was a young French woman staying. She must have been
nineteen, and it was a pen-pal, student-exchange scheme with
some of their old SAS allies in the Châtillon region, where they
were dropped post D-Day to carve a path for the Yanks in 1944,
and cause bother.

The Maquis, they were called, these French allies. Resistance
fighters, really.

Well, in the early 80s, the SAS mob were invited over to
Châtillon and were honoured for their part, and this led to the
student-exchange scheme, not that I ever benefited.

There's an award, a certificate, I suppose it is, when all's said and
done, hanging on the wall in my flat, from the Maquis, honouring
my grandad, specifically, for what he did in and around Châtillon
in 1944. It's right next to the one from The People of Norway
thanking him for his role in 'helping to restore freedom to our
land'.

Good lads.

Anyway, in the early 80s I was only a kid, when this nineteen-
year-old French woman plonked me on her lap. I soon squirmed
away.

Tanky grabbed me, gave me a little tap to the side of the head.

'You want your bonce examining, my old son,' he said, grinning.
He nodded over at Delphine, or Claudette, or Mathilde, or Alice,

or Nicolette, or whatever her sexy little name was, and said, 'Few years from now you'll be trying to climb on, not jump off.'

Everyone laughed.

Doris, Tanky's wife, she laughed. My grandad laughed. Delphine or Claudette, or Mathilde, or Alice, or Nicolette laughed.

My grandma didn't laugh.

Good old Tanky.

Three

'Lying on my back, smoking a cigarette and stroking her hair, I thought: what a life for a soldier!'

'Same again, Harry?'

Wilf Gardiner points at Challenor's bottle of brown ale.

'Go on then,' Challenor says. 'In for a penny, eh, Wilf.'

'In for a penny.'

Wilf Gardiner has a whisky glass bunched in his fat fist. He knocks it against Challenor's new bottle of brown ale, and the ice clinks and a few drops of the whisky slither over the top of the glass and run down over Gardiner's fat fingers and Challenor makes a good show of wiping his own hand on his trousers.

'My mistake,' Gardiner says. 'Apologies, Harry.'

'It happens,' Challenor says. 'It can happen to the best of us, Wilf. No harm, no foul.'

'Well, cheers, anyway,' Gardiner says, and he pours whisky from his fat fist straight down his fat neck. 'Good health.'

Challenor's head bobs. He clocks the clientele. It's not heaving, really, for a Thursday, a Thursday in late September. End of the summer, he thinks. There is a hubbub, a low one, and radio's playing 'Soldier Boy' by The Shirelles, a group that Challenor admires. He listens to the song as Gardiner barks instructions at some of his yobs. They're a ham-faced, tight-mouthed, thick-necked lot, Wilf Gardiner's yobs. Not the brightest of sparks, Challenor suspects, these men brought up in and around pubs, clubs, bookies, these men working as Wilf Gardiner's yobs. The Shirelles turn Challenor's ear. They're singing about how they'll never make their fella blue, that there's only ever one girl, only one girl you can love.

Challenor reckons he's only ever really loved but one girl. He's had his moments, of course he has, young good-looking soldier like Challenor, a good-looking soldier boy himself, hasn't been short of moments, but love, *love*, well, there's only ever been but one girl.

The yobs are shifting crates to and from the bar area.

'What can I do you for, Harry?' Gardiner asks.

'I've just been talking to your missus.'

'Oh yeah?'

'Yeah.'

'Get any sense out of her? I rarely do.'

Challenor frowns. 'I must say, Wilf, I suspect that this is more a reflection of your failures as a conversationalist than it is hers.'

'All right, Harry, easy on,' Gardiner says, raising a palm. 'You've a good point. She's a fine woman. Just having a crack, know what I mean.'

'Yes, I know what those words mean.'

'So?'

'So she's filled me in on how your nonsense with Oliva and Ford and Pedrini and so on really started.'

'Oh she has, has she?'

'She has.'

Gardiner's nodding. 'Well, it's not like I've lied to you, Harry, is it?'

'I suppose not.'

'What's next then?'

Straight to the point, Challenor thinks. I'll say that for you, Wilf – you're always straight to the point when you're caught out and you need a solution. I *will* say that for you.

'A thought, Wilf, occurred.'

Gardiner is nodding again. 'The starting point isn't really the point, though is it?' he says. 'The start has led us here, that's all. Here, where you want us to be, right?'

'The Italians threaten you. They've threatened your missus. There's your corroboration, you know, for the legal lot, for *court*, when it comes to it.'

Gardiner catches on. 'Gotcha,' he says.

'We need a caught-red-handed scenario, really, for our Italian friends, understand, for me to go to work.'

'Okey doke. When?'

'Tomorrow: Friday. September twenty-first, it is. Or will be. That works.' Challenor turns his bottle of beer, peels at the label on his bottle of beer. 'That do you?'

'That'll work, Harry.'

'Good. Set it up for about eleven p.m. OK?'

'And what do I tell them?'

'That you're game, you're in, that you'll do what they ask – what they *say*. You tell them that, and when they turn up, you let them see that this, in fact, is simply not true.'

Gardiner's still nodding. 'Gotcha.'

'And keep the missus well away tomorrow night, you know, just in case.'

'Will do.'

Challenor drains his bottle of brown ale. 'It'll be two new lads, Wilf, understand? So you won't recognise them. Police Constables Legge and Wells.'

'Gotcha.'

'And I'll see you after, at the Mad House, and we knock this little palaver on the head once and for all.'

'Suits me, Harry.'

Challenor stands. He leans forward. He means business,

Challenor. He does *not* mess about. His head is inches from Gardiner's fat face. Challenor smiles. 'And after we've done and knocked it all on the *head*, you and me will have a proper chat about how you can help me a bit better, help me do my job with a little bit more efficiency, Wilf.' He straightens up. 'That suit you too, Wilf?'

Gardiner nods. Gardiner does not look thrilled by this news. He is not, Challenor thinks, tickled by this prospect.

'You know how it is, Harry,' he says. 'I'd love to help, but if I ain't got socks, I can hardly pull them up now, can I?'

Challenor grins. '*Arrivederci*,' he says.

*

'You don't say much do you, sir,' you say to Thomas Macleggan Wedderburn, your senior officer on this Italian job –

Blowing up trains in tunnels.

Here the two of you are, you a working-class tyke from a none-too-happy home, he a posh Jock law student in owlish glasses. 'Tojo', you reckon, makes a good little nickname for Lieutenant Wedderburn –

You wonder how long until you'll be able to use it.

Bit cheeky, of course, imagining your senior officer looks like a general in the Japanese Imperial Army.

'There's not much to say, lad,' Wedderburn says.

'I suppose not,' you reply.

'There'll be plenty to talk about when we find our targets, Tanky.'

You nod. You'd found a bridge the night before, but there was no chance you had enough explosives to do that over, so you left it.

You're on day five now, slogging on, trudging on, night after night, sleeping a little each day, when you can, under whatever bush or brush or copse offers any sort of shelter.

It's a lonely business.

*

Challenor leaves the Phoenix. He heads back to the Geisha. He's got an idea, something he does not want Wilf Gardiner to know about, seeing as it'll throw a spanner in the business the next evening, September 21st. He needs to speak to Elizabeth Ewing Evans. Just a quick word –

Just needs to get hold of some contact information.

*

You know that the Apennine mountains running down the spine of Italy, are, in fact, the spine of Italy, look, even on a map, like the spine of Italy –

The cracked vertebrae, the twisted bone structure of the spine of Italy.

And you know that you were dropped somewhere near the northernmost part of the Appennino Centrale mountains. And you know that somewhere a little to your west is La Spezia. And you know that somewhere a little to your east is Bologna. And you know that there is a significant railway line that runs between the two cities. And you know that to get through the Appennino Centrale mountains, these trains have to, they simply have to, there is nothing else for it, they have to go through tunnels to make their important goods runs between La Spezia and Bologna.

So why is it, you think, hour after hour, day after day, night after night, for six days and six nights now, why is it, you think, time and again, why is it that you can't find a single fucking trace of a tunnel in these mountains?

Where are these fucking tunnels? you ask yourself, hour after hour, night after night tramping around in the dark.

Where are they? you ask yourself, day after day, lying in a bush, a shrub, trying to sleep, but not sleeping as the question echoes and ricochets –

And then: day seven –

*

Challenor leaves the Geisha club with two addresses and a phone number written on a scrap of paper.

He looks at his watch. It is almost midnight. He weighs it –

No chance now of finding what he needs, *who* he needs.

Doris has been calling him The Stranger. No need to guess why. He pauses for a moment on Charing Cross Road, watches the traffic shunt by Cambridge Circus, watches the late night Soho crowd throb in down Moor Street, past the Spice of Life, up Romilly towards the Coach and Horses, which will still be open, quietly enough, locked in, yes, but still open to those who know how to get in the side door. Challenor thinks he might pop in, could pop into the Coach and Horses, for a quick one, and if he keeps his head down, he can well easily get a quick one in before causing any bother, and it's already midnight, so he's still The Stranger either way.

Yeah, quick one, go on then.

*

'And on the seventh day…'

Well, Tojo laughs at that one. 'Tell you what, Tanky, it's about bloody time, right? Let's get to work. First thing's first: we need to see if it's safe.'

By safe you know Tojo means sentry-free. 'I'll go,' you say, in a heartbeat.

Tojo is nodding. 'See up there?' He points to a tree that is bent, bent over and into another tree, about fifty yards up the mountainside, providing cover, shelter. You nod. Tojo continues, 'I'll take the packs, the kit, and wait up there. New base, got it?'

You nod. 'Yes, sir,' you say.

68

'*Go on then, lad.*'

You go. You slip down the mountain, dead quiet. Your army-issue knife is in your hand, ready to strike at the enemy, to pierce from behind the heart of any sentry.

Here we go, you think, here we fucking go —

You fancy yourself as a silent killer.

The mountain's lighter down here, towards the tunnel, the dark hills roll into paths, shallower ground, turf flattened by livestock — what, sheep? Goats? — trees sharper, tidier, more domesticated it seems. A stream runs alongside the railway line and you step into it, you need to cross it to get to the entrance of the tunnel. You're stepping alongside the line down in the river, down here in Italy, falling, ghosting into the shadows the trees afford, your movement blends in, you are these shadows, these shadows become you, a ghost, you become a ghost, a silent killer, any noise deadened by the splashing and gurgling of the stream.

You reach the mouth of the tunnel. You can't hear anything beyond the gurgle and splash of the stream and the rustle of the wind through the leaves of these sharper, tidier trees down here. The mouth of the tunnel is a gaping hole of black, grey stones showing the faint light of the ground. On the other side of the track, the ground rolls away, down a touch, and then rises again. You are in a dip, a valley, and you can see no sign of any fucker, sentry or otherwise.

You know what they say about sentries though —

If they're not where they should be, they'll be having a snout half a yard behind you, so watch your fucking back.

You watch your fucking back. You give it a few snouts' worth, time-wise, and decide to take a proper look.

The tunnel is long, long, long, and dark like a cellar, and cold like charity. It's damp, and the drips echo. Two lines, one up, one down, and you realise you and Tojo can do some serious damage here, if you get enough time to set the charges at either end.

And there is no one. There are no sentries. It occurs that perhaps there's a reason –

Why the fuck would anyone be here, *down here, so far behind the lines? Isn't that the point of the mission?*

Either way, there are no sentries and you are deflated. There's not been a real hitch, not been a chance to have a go.

Tojo's happy, though.

*

Challenor sits at his desk. He stares at his desk. His head thrums. His head throbs. His head spins. His head, to be honest, really honest, if he really thinks about it, his head feels like it's been turned upside down, *inside.*

It feels as if his brains are in his fucking *chin.*

It's early –

Well, if he really thinks about it, it's still late. It's quite late, he thinks, which makes it quite early. It's neither really early or really late yet. He reckons he'll hit both in about half an hour, if he stays exactly where he is, stays at his desk, not moving, staring at it. If he does that, it'll be really late and really early at exactly the same time and this should help, this should really *help.* Christ, it'll be *helpful* when the time sorts itself out, when it's worked out what it is, the time, early or late.

Radio's on. Some jingle jangle about Sheila, sweet little Sheila.

Someone walks past Challenor's office. 'Oi,' he shouts, 'oi, you! Get in here!'

Police Sergeant Alan Ratcliffe pokes his head round the door. 'Guv?'

'Oh, hello, Alan, it's you.'

'Sir?' Police Sergeant Alan Ratcliffe looks confused.

Challenor isn't sure how to help him regarding this confusion, though Challenor recognises that he's confused, and that feels like something, like an achievement, some *understanding* at least.

Challenor nods, eyebrows raised, at the ceiling, indicating the music that is jangling through his office. He says, 'I thought Buddy Holly had bloody died.'

'Sir?'

Challenor is nodding, fast, and he realises that Police Sergeant Alan Ratcliffe remains confused. 'The song, Alan, that's playing.' Ratcliffe now nods himself. 'Is it not Buddy Holly, Alan?'

'It's not, no, guv.'

'Well who is it, Alan?'

'It's a Yank, guv, I think, a lad name of Tommy Roe.'

'Is it now.'

Challenor's head bobs. He starts to laugh. He starts to convulse with laughter.

'Sir?' Ratcliffe asks. He looks a little nervous, does Police Sergeant Alan Ratcliffe. Challenor recognises the look that his subordinates sometimes have on their nervous little faces.

Challenor raises a palm. 'Well, Alan, this Tommy Roe, we ought to get him down here, we ought to nick him, this Tommy Roe, nick him and book him, Alan.'

Challenor continues to laugh, continues to convulse, to shake with laughter.

'Sir?'

''Cos he's a thief, Alan!' Challenor delivers the punchline between gasps, gleeful gasps. 'He's stitched Buddy Holly right up with this little number. Done a real number on him, in fact, Alan. Get it, Alan? Get it?'

'I think so, sir, yes.'

'On you go, Alan, as you were.' Challenor waves Ratcliffe away. His laughter settles, his shaking settles, his convulsions settle. He says, to himself, 'Poor old Buddy Holly, bloody shame that was.'

He wipes his eyes. He grimaces. His head *sings*. His head *yells*.

Christ it's early, he thinks. And he has a big day, a long day ahead of him. The previous night's drinking was, he now accepts, something of a mistake.

*

'Christ it's dark in here, Tanky,' Wedderburn says, as you inch along, deeper into the tunnel, like blind men it's so dark, using the line, tapping the line, to keep your bearings, the line your white stick. 'We better get a wriggle on.'

You know that there tend to be lengthy enough intervals between trains – you've been timing them – and you know that the majority of these trains are goods trains, and this is good news.

You know this, but it doesn't half make time slow down when you're laying charges in a tunnel. And if you don't do it sharpish, gawd knows what'll come out of the gloom and smash you to smithereens, really do a number on you, an ironic little number.

One hundred yards in, and you lay the charges against the 'down' line from Pontremoli. It takes you five minutes. It feels like hours, like hours and hours in the dark, as you shake and shiver from the cold and the nerves and the fear, the fear of a train –

And Christ it's hard work, fiddly work, laying charges against the line like this when it's so dark and so cold.

You burrow deeper into the tunnel. You cross to the other side of the tunnel. You lay charges on the 'up' line. The 'up' line, you believe, runs towards La Spezia.

It takes about five minutes to lay these charges on the 'up' line.

'Come on, Tanky, well done,' Wedderburn says. 'Let's get out of here.'

You move as fast as you can. But it's dark, and it's cold, and it's damp, and each step is a hindrance, really, each step stops you from going faster, from walking freely, and it's a bloody nightmare, and then the line starts to hum, to fizz, to warm up, and you know what this means.

The line hums louder. The line sings –

'Good God,' says Wedderburn. 'Move, man. Run like hell.'

The line yells –

You're already running, sprinting. You don't need a senior officer to tell you that. And what's odd is that suddenly you can *run, suddenly it feels like you can move, you can get out.*

You're racing the train –

Head on.

You need to get out of the tunnel before it gets in, before it hits you in the face, punches you slap in the face, headbutts your face with its face –

You have the peace of mind to decide that, yes, this is the way round: you'd rather hit the fucker head on than have it plough into your back.

The circle of light ahead gets bigger, the noise of the tracks thrums louder, and the chug of the train is more persistent, more prominent.

And then you're in the stream, you're soaked as you've dived head first into the stream –

Just quickly enough to see a goods train, running towards La Spezia, you believe, disappear into the mouth of the tunnel.

*

The previous night Challenor went into the Coach and Horses via the lock-in entrance and proceeded to drink four bottles of brown ale and four whiskies very quickly.

He was halfway through his third bottle when someone clocked him, and there were a few murmurings, which he fronted out, and then a group dispersed as he purchased bottle number four, and then the same group gathered around him as he drank bottle number four and suggested he might want to leave.

Challenor remembers, now, staring at his desk, early, very early in the morning, that he wasn't too keen on leaving.

Before leaving the Coach and Horses, Challenor swore violent revenge on at least half of the small group that had dispersed and then gathered around him to persuade him to leave, and then he put a chair through the window.

Well, he thinks now, with a wry grin – and this wry grin seems encouraging, he thinks, in terms of his imminent recovery – he didn't put it *through* the window exactly, as the chair bounced back and landed, upright, ready for use, back inside the saloon. Challenor was not the only patron present to be surprised by this turn of events. The group that were gathered around him – two of whom had had to move sharpish to avoid this chair – stared in disbelief at the chair's new position.

Challenor chuckles now at what happened next.

He, Challenor, sat down on the chair.

The group looked hard at the window.

Challenor sighed and smiled and waved his fourth bottle of brown ale at the bar staff, clearly desiring another.

The group looked at Challenor.

Challenor said, 'Pull up a pew, have a seat, it's bloody raining them, after all!'

The group looked again at the window.

Challenor said, 'It's not fucking rocket science, my old darlings!'

The window, it turned out, was open, and Challenor's chair had in fact bounced back off the shutters which had been pulled down so as not to alert the long arm of the law to the illegal drinking that was going on.

Challenor smiles now as he remembers enjoying explaining that avoiding the police meant there was no damage. Had he, Challenor, not been around that evening, there would have been no need to pull down the shutters.

The pub was not wholly convinced by this explanation, by its logic.

Challenor did not stay much longer.

After he left the Coach and Horses, via the side door, he turned right, right again, and right again, to find himself back on Moor Street. While he had had a fair wallop of booze, he was smart enough not to return to the Geisha. He smiles at this foresight now, staring at his desk, his head smarting despite these smarts, his head *bellowing*, in general complaint.

Instead, Challenor barged into Limoncello, his favourite Soho trattoria, where his old pal Lucky 'Luke' Luciano was tidying away and chin-wagging with the staff. They were not, Challenor understands now, thrilled to see him. They were not at all tickled by his appearance, this was clear from the word go.

Their hospitality was brief, but significant: a bottle of the restaurant's eponymous spirit was lifted out from behind the bar and several large measures were poured first into a tumbler, and second down Challenor's throat.

Cheers, Algiers; Algiers, cheers! He remembers toasting the room with this to a general bewilderment. Challenor knew his friend's game: sink him with fortified drink and he'll be out of your hair all the quicker.

And Lucky Luke was right.

*

Face down in the stream, it occurs that the train would not have hit you in the face, would not have headbutted your face with its face, as there was plenty of room on the other side of the tunnel to avoid that fate, that face.

Of course – you were running as the charges you laid would have gone off inside the tunnel with you in it, and there is no way you would have avoided that fate, as you now can tell by the wrench of metal, the screech of metal against rock.

Fuck me, it worked. Smoke rolls, avalanches from the mouth of the tunnel. Flames flash. Parts of the train go bang, explode, crack.

You mention your little misunderstanding to Tojo.

'Haha, you wally, Tanky,' he says, 'but whatever gets you out in time, right?'

That God's honest, you think.

Then you hear it: a low thrum, a hum, the line is buzzing *again.*

'Christ,' Tojo says, 'there's one coming the other way!'

And then the crunch, and the screech, and the wrench, but you don't wait around to inspect your handiwork, you scramble the fuck up the hill to your hideout and try and put as much distance as you can between you and it, your handiwork.

You smile, thinking of a nickname for you both:

Two Train Tojo and Tanky –

Who dares wins.

*

It's still very early, or very late –

Challenor clocks this ambiguity he feels and understands that it means he is not ready for anything more than his office, his desk, just yet. This is a big day, a long day that he has in front of him and it is important that he sets himself about it the right way, and, at this early – or late – point in the day recuperation is the key. He must, he accepts, recuperate, recover. But what *from*?

Himself, he supposes –

He needs to recover from himself.

Challenor charged out of Lucky Luke's charged up by a good dose of fortification, of fuel –

And then didn't know what to do next.

It's quite the problem in Soho for your drinker who isn't especially keen on either live music or live ladies. Challenor likes music, he's listening to it now after all, he thinks, but he likes it on his own terms. Whenever he has tried to enjoy the live music experience, there have been moments of great pleasure, of euphoria, even, when he has been swept up in the rhythm, the swing, the sweet voice and the hard, percussive *sway*, when he's looked about him and seen a joyous bunch of youngsters, face-splitting grins on them all, and he's reckoned he's understood this live music lark. And then he's needed to go for a slash, and to do so has meant fighting his way across a packed dance floor, a packed, sweaty, writhing, jumping dance floor past a load of twelve-year-olds full of hair grease and he thinks, perhaps I don't need this live music lark after all.

So where does your drinker go then?

Challenor tried Trisha's on Greek Street. He got halfway down the stairs before the pair of berks who run the door picked him up by his arms and carried him back out.

'Go home, Harry,' one of the berks had said. 'It's four in the morning and we're closed.'

'Home? At four?' he'd replied. 'I'm going to *work*, my old darling.'

And after that, he remembers now, he did the one thing he should really regret –

He shunted his way, bull-like, up through Soho to West End Central, the Mad House. And at the Mad House, he went down to the holding cells. And in one of the holding cells he found a young lad, whose name he forgets. This young lad was brought in for causing a spot at a local skin shop on Berwick Street. This lad had, it transpires, been bothering an employee of this skin shop. The police constable on duty informed Challenor that the young lad was a known associate of Joseph Oliva, one of his mob, low down the chain of command, but still. Challenor told the Police

Constable on duty to let him into the cell. In the cell, he took out a piece of lead piping that was in the inside pocket of his coat. He dropped this on the floor next to the young lad.

'That's yours,' he said to the lad.

He then took the lad by the lapels and slapped him about the face. He gripped him by the throat and slapped him about the face. He pushed him up against the wall and drove the palm of his hand repeatedly against the wall, just to the right of the young lad's head. The wall crumbled.

'Who's is the lead, son?' he asked. His eyes flashed. 'You crummy little sod. I'm sure I've knocked you off before. Receiving, wasn't it? I'll have you again, too, you'll see.'

He breathed alcohol like a dragon. He stuck his face in the young lad's face. He carried the lad to the wall on the opposite side of the cell. He pinned the lad up against this wall by the throat with his left forearm. With the palm of his right hand, he pushed at – he *massaged*, really – the forehead of the young lad into the wall. The wall scratched under the weight. The wall balked under the weight. The young lad trembled. The young lad said nothing. The young lad gasped –

Challenor heard the tell-tale trickle of urine on cell floor. Job done.

After a little while, Challenor put the young lad down and picked up the lead piping.

'I'll deliver this to the duty officer, then, lad. Seeing as I've discovered it on your person, during my interrogation.' He grinned at this unfortunate lad. 'Mind how you go, my old darling,' he said.

Yes, he thinks now, his head screaming, his head really *bickering* with him, this is the one thing he should really regret. Thing is, he doesn't –

He doesn't regret it at all.

Who dares wins, he thinks.

*

You're heading higher and higher into the mountains and further and further south towards Pontremoli –

Rendezvous with Dudgeon and the other lads. You should make it.

Your knees are bleeding. Your arms are bleeding. You fall and you pick yourself up, you scramble and you sweat, you bend under the weight of your pack, your equipment. You climb higher and higher. The air thin. The rocks jagged –

These Italian mountains craggy and beautiful in the cool of the night, as the sun comes up, the red sun illuminates the edges of these mountains, and you think they're not so different to the Highlands of Scotland in their edge of wildness, in their edge.

And you're driven on, partly by the thought of meeting the other lads – you'll get some bloody conversation out of some of them – and partly as you're excited, you're like a child, ready to share your success.

Wedderburn leads. He's got the map, the compass, the bearing, and, well the bearing, that officer bearing.

'See that church, Tanky, down by the stream?'

You nod.

'That's Villafranca,' he points north, 'just up there, and that's La Spezia,' he points west, 'so that must be the church.'

You've no argument. There's an issue though.

'We're going to have to leave the cover of the mountains,' Wedderburn says. 'Make a break for the lower ground. I suspect we won't be alone down there.'

This is no issue, you think. This you relish.

'Let's get on with it, Tanky.' Wedderburn folds the map. You finger your knife. 'Quicker we get down there, quicker we know.'

Sounds good to you. The pair of you are lean, hungry, dirty, sweaty, bearded –

Killers.

*You reach the point on the map, the agreed rendezvous point, on the
bank of the stream, a little down from the church.
You're definitely in the right place –
Thing is, no one else seems to be.*

*

Challenor looks at the two addresses on the scrap of paper –
Miracle I didn't lose this, he thinks.

His head sighs. His head exhales. His head *deflates*.

He thinks it's about time he did a little work, also that it's about
time he did a little work, looking at the clock and seeing that it is
8.30 a.m., and that he has been asleep face down on his desk for
the last forty-seven minutes. He snorts, clears his nose and throat,
gives it the old smoker's hello, hacking and snorting, he is, for a few
minutes. The coffee he had one of his nervous subordinates go and
fetch him about an hour ago – or did a nervous subordinate bring
it without his prompting? It's possible, but if so, he'll have words
– is beside him and loaded with sugar and thick with cream, and
cold, cold with a filthy layer of skin on the top of it. He skims his
finger over this layer of skin and pulls it out, and carefully drops it
in his bin. Soho, he thinks, is all about *skin*: skin flicks, skin shops,
skin shows. Skin you alive, it will, Soho. Skin-of-your-teeth type
of scene, he thinks, Soho. *The Soho skin crawl will make your skin
crawl.* No other way through. Soho is a cold, cold, thick cup of
coffee, old and unwanted, charged with caffeine, with *fuel*, dark
and murky, with a nasty, sorry, unfortunate layer of skin on the top.

What are you going to do about it?

Well, the first thing he's going to do today is head down to one of
the addresses on his scrap of paper. A Georgian gaff in Bloomsbury
where, he believes, a certain Josephine Jennings resides, a young
woman who, he's been told, can sometimes be seen out dancing

with old Riccardo Pedrini. She'll do, he thinks, she'll do as a start-ing point for today. There is still a little under fifteen hours until kick-off tonight, so there is plenty of time to brief some of the minor players and ensure the match is weighted nicely in his favour.

He decides to walk. His head could do with air, he thinks, could do with the exercise, his head. He really thinks his head will benefit from the walk, will appreciate it. He should take his head out walking more often, during the day, he considers. He walks at night too much, and his head misses the sunshine, the rays of sun, those life-giving rays. When he started at the Flying Squad, and when he and Doris lived in Mitcham, he would walk home, some nights, most nights, hour and a half it took, sometimes more, but what a way to keep his head clear, and to keep in shape too.

He sets out, his head down as he leaves the Mad House. He doesn't want any grief for the thing he did that he doesn't regret. There'll be a court hearing soon enough and he'll stand up and say what he always says and the fact is that the lad is a pest, a whore-botherer, and we don't like them, and a known associate of Mr Oliva to boot, so Brass won't be at all upset if the lad gets slapped with a heavy fine, or even does a little stretch, a month or so, just for show, as that's why he, Challenor, was brought in, clear through some of this Soho murk, sieve the place of murk, and make the whole place a little more palatable, a little more drinkable.

He charges down Oxford Street. Easier this way, less criminal dis-traction on Oxford Street. Does a left up Tottenham Court Road, then a right straight off, and then wriggles through into Bedford Square. Late September, he thinks. He takes a seat on a bench on the street in Bedford Square, and decides he'll wait until after 9 a.m. He reckons it's not really on to pay a visit to a civilian before 9 a.m., you don't want to worry them, after all, unnecessarily, especially if you're hoping they'll do something for you.

Late September. It doesn't know what it's about, the weather, in late September. It's fresh, he'll give it that, this late-September day. He'll let today have that, certainly. Fresh, clear, thin air. He doesn't get too much thin air around here, these days. There's a chill to it, too, the day. Late September sun is, what? Not quite autumn, too weak a proposition to be summer. It's schizophrenic, really, this weather, this sun, doesn't know what it's about, warm one moment, cool the next, the sun just doesn't know what it is in late September, won't make its mind up.

There are leaves starting to fall, he notices, about the place. There's a grey, light haze to the square. Josephine Jennings lives just off the square, not far from the Pedrini clan, and he wonders if this is a childhood romance situation. Certainly they've been seen dancing at the Lorraine club, and that's not on Challenor's radar as an especially naughty venue. Not quite wholesome – no, he wouldn't say it was wholesome – but it's attended, generally, by good kids, and appears not to be a front for anything. Which is rare, but not unheard of.

The square is waking up. Doors open, men skip down steps to work. Men skip up other steps and doors open and in they go to work. Funny old place, Bedford Square, he thinks –

Dual-personality type thing going on, in some senses. If you can ascribe such a diagnosis, such a sentiment, to a place. There's likely a book term for this, he thinks. Old Tojo'd know. He smiles. Course he would. He'd have known, for sure. He was quite the bookworm, old Tojo. He hasn't thought of Lieutenant Wedderburn for some time. He's not sure his head is up to it today, if he's honest. So he shakes it, his head, and checks his watch and, seeing it's after nine, he heads across the square to locate the domicile of one Josephine Jennings.

*

'I can't keep doing this, Tanky,' Tojo says. 'This hide and seek is killing me.'

You know how he feels. You're crawling up the mountain before first light to hide, and then crawling down again as it gets dark. Up and down, down and up for two days and two nights. Carrying everything with you each time you go up and down.

And still no one –

On the third day, Tojo says, 'Fuck it, let's just roll our sleeping bags here and be done with it. At least something might happen.'

You're in for a penny there, you think. And Tojo never swears. So the pair of you bunk down in a ditch not far from the rendezvous point. You conk out like a milk-drunk baby.

And then –

The sun dazzling, the stream dancing, you wake up with what you know is a heavy boot, nudging you in the ribs.

*

'Don't worry,' Challenor says to Josephine Jennings's concerned-looking mother. 'She's not done anything wrong, nothing at all.'

Mrs Jennings has a thin-lipped, furrowed-brow face on, topped off by a puckered mouth and narrowed eyes. She hands Challenor a muddy, grimy-looking cup of coffee.

'I thought I'd pop round your drum directly, have a quiet word, you know,' Challenor says, giving it the local bobby. 'Don't want to put you out.'

She says, tentatively, 'You won't mind if I stay put then, Detective Challenor? For the interview?'

Challenor's head hums. His head *whirrs*. He can feel the caffeine course with each sip of this muddy, grimy coffee. He gives Mrs Jennings a serious, strained sort of smile. He does not have to act in any way to administer this smile.

He says, 'It's not an interview, Mrs Jennings, just a word about some people your daughter may know, some friends of friends, if you like.' He pauses, delivers another serious, contemplative look, and adds, 'I think it's best we have a little privacy. It'll be a moment, maybe two, no more, and there's really no need for you to worry.'

Mrs Jennings presents Challenor with a serious, concerned look of her own. 'Very well,' she says, all timid. She gives her daughter's hand a squeeze and then, well, Challenor thinks, the word he's after is *retires*. She gives her daughter's hand a squeeze and she retires.

Challenor's head *races*. His head is scampering about all over the gaff. It's like a bloody lab rat, now, Challenor's head.

Josephine Jennings is a cool-looking customer. She certainly seems unfazed, indifferent, even, Challenor thinks.

'How can I help you, detective?' she asks.

'Clever girl,' Challenor says.

'No need for that, detective.'

'No need for what?'

'Patronising. No need to be patronising.'

Challenor grins. His head zips. His head *grins*. 'Point taken,' he says. 'But it is *somewhat* smart of you, insightful, really, to offer, you know, your help, straight off the bat, I mean, first up. Clever.'

'Seems like the best use of our time. Speed things along.'

'OK, Josephine, I'll get straight to the point.'

'Please do.'

'Right so, the point. I've heard you knock about with Riccardo Pedrini. That true?'

Josephine Jennings smiles. 'Knock about with?'

'OK,' Challenor says, 'I've heard that you occasionally frequent certain Soho establishments together.'

'*That* is true, yes.'

'Right. So you know his pal Joseph Oliva?'

'I wouldn't say I *know* him. He's sometimes around.'

'Right, gotcha. Know his reputation, do you?'

Josephine raises her eyebrows. She smiles again. 'I've heard him refer to himself as "King" Oliva.' Challenor can hear the irony. Josephine's smile brightens. 'I'm not sure that's quite the same thing, though, is it? Not sure it answers your question, exactly.'

Challenor smirks. 'How long have you known Pedrini?'

'On and off, years.'

'And young Maria, his cousin. Know her, do you?'

'*Met* her.'

'Right, OK. I'll get to the point.'

'You've said that.'

Challenor rolls his eyes. His head *twangs*. Someone is plucking some string that's pulled tight, right through the middle of his bonce. Taut as fuck this string is, twanging away it is, twanging away in the middle of his pulsing bonce.

'You OK, detective?'

'Nothing a body transplant wouldn't fix,' he says.

Josephine Jennings smirks.

'Age,' Challenor adds. 'It's a tricky fucker, age. A hell of a leveller, age, you'll find, one day.'

'Yes.'

'Relentless, it is. No hiding from it, age.'

'Anyway…'

Challenor nods. 'Right, the *point*. I need you to do something for me, and you will do it because although I know you have nothing to do with anything, you know, *naughty*, we are looking at *known associates* of Oliva's, and,' he pauses, '*knocking about* with old Pedrini is quite enough of a thing to mean an easy transition from outside the circle to in it, if you know what I mean.' He pauses again. 'We clear?'

Josephine Jennings is nodding. 'Crystal,' she says.

'I want you to tell Pedrini, *today*, as in *soon*, two things. Firstly, I want you to tell him that I've been sniffing about.'

'Which is true.'

'Which is true. Secondly, I want you to tell him that I told you that if they – and by "they" you know who I mean – ' Josephine Jennings nods '– if they don't nail old Wilf Gardiner down pronto, then old Wilf Gardiner's thinking about giving me young Maria on a solicitation number.'

'Which is not true.'

'Clever girl.'

'Like you said.'

'So?'

'I can do that,' Josephine Jennings says. 'And what about me?'

'You're passing on a message – also true. And that's it.'

'That's it? Nothing else you're going to make me do?'

'Not a prosciutto sausage more, sweetheart.'

Josephine Jennings smiles. 'I'll see you out,' she says.

At the door, Challenor says, 'Oh, and if you see them tonight – and you likely should, you know, keep everything above board and so on – be aware that come the end of the evening, I expect they'll be headed to the Phoenix club on Old Compton Street. Know it?'

Josephine Jennings nods. 'Skin joint, right? One of Mr Gardiner's?'

'That's the badger.'

Josephine Jennings nods.

'I'd steer clear,' Challenor says, and he skips down the steps, off to work.

His head, he thinks, his head *aches*.

*

Your hand is on your Schmeisser and your knife is hidden inside your sleeping bag –

Easy reach. Easy does it.

The sun blinds you.

'Easy, Tanky,' you hear Tojo mutter.

First thing's first – you realise very quickly that this isn't one of your mob.

Second thing, you clock that the man with his foot in your side is alone. He's alone, and he is very rustic looking, you realise. In fact, you think, as you lie, unblinking but blinded, unmoving, if, one month ago, someone had asked you to describe what you reckon an Italian peasant farmer might look like, you reckon you would have described something very similar indeed to the man standing above you, grinning, with his foot lodged in your side.

He looks at you in something like astonishment, amused astonishment, or what you expect passes for astonishment with rustic, stoic, Italian, peasant farmers. A sort of stoic indifference, just about quizzical.

He looks at you in something like astonishment and says, 'Inglesi?'

You laugh. 'So much for our uniforms then,' you say to Tojo. Your uniforms, you remember, are supposed to resemble the German uniforms.

'Shut up, Tanky,' Tojo says.

Tojo and the Italian begin to engage in some hand waving and tentative chat. Sounds like more than one language to you. Either way, you lie still, one hand on your Schmeisser, the other wrapped around your knife.

A conversation, of sorts, ensues. In French, you think? Can't be. You think: get a fucking wriggle on, Tojo. The longer we're here, the quicker we're fucked –

Nerves. You're not afraid, but you're nervous, and when you're nervous you twitch, you race, you act –

'Come on, Tanky,' Tojo says, 'we're going for a feed.'

You slip out of your sleeping bag and gather your things.

Now this turn of events, you decide, is very good news indeed.

*

Challenor rings the bell of a fairly well-to-do Georgian town house in Bloomsbury.

A young woman – a girl, really – answers the door.

'You Maria?' Challenor asks.

The girl curls her lip. 'No.'

'Who are you then?'

'I'm her sister,' she says. 'Wait – you from school?'

Challenor laughs. 'You supposed to be there then?'

The girl shrugs. 'You know.'

'I'm a detective, young lady. Detective Sergeant Harold Challenor.'

'The school sent a detective? Blimey.'

'Gawdsake,' Challenor says. 'Where's your sister?'

'She'll be in the church. You know the one on Clerkenwell Road? Roman Catholic one?'

'I know it. What's she doing in there then?'

'You know the delicatessen next door? Terroni's?'

'I do know it, yes.'

The girl pulls a chirpy, proud, *so-there* face. 'My family's that is. She works today. Says the church is the only place she ever gets any peace and quiet.'

'Hard worker then.'

The girl sticks out her tongue.

'Charming.' Challenor grins. 'Your cousin Riccardo in today?'

'Nah, at least not until late this afternoon.'

'Not an early riser then?'

The girl laughs. 'I wouldn't know. He doesn't live *here*.'

'Where *does* he live?'

The girl pushes the door slightly to, aware, Challenor realises, that she's saying too much, perhaps, though also that she's confused, as she clearly knows nothing about her cousin. There's that instinct, Challenor knows it well, that instinct that even your civilians will have round here, in the older families, that instinct to keep your gob shut when there's a copper asking questions. She's got it, Challenor can see that. Just the slight touch on the door, and the closing of the expression, the slight darkening. Not so playful now, she's not.

Challenor reads all this in a flash. No point getting her into trouble.

'Don't worry your pretty little head about it, girl,' he says. 'We'll keep this little *conversazione* to ourselves.'

The girl raises her eyebrows. 'How come you speak Italian?' she asks.

Challenor winks. 'Long story, girl.'

*

You're following the Italian peasant farmer and the bugger's only bloody grinning, grinning like a bloody loony –

He keeps turning, beckoning to you, to follow him, and he's still grinning, and turning and bending his dirty, soiled little farmer's finger, beckoning you with it, and you never do know, so you keep your Schmeisser handy and your knife unsheathed.

But Tojo seems OK with it all, and he's having a chin wag with the old lad in French, you reckon, and you're gasping for some tuck, some wine and some scran, a full belly would change pretty much any situation, but right now, gawd Jesus, you could really do with a feed and a bloody lie-down on something soft.

The farm is a square-brick house with a few primitive barns dotted about the place that look lively for a bit of shelter, you think.

And then you're following him inside to a big flag-stoned kitchen with great long beams running above you, and each bloody great long beam has got a whole load of bloody hams hanging from it, each of these bloody long beams is festooned *with hams –*

Festooned they are!

And your stomach doesn't half flip at the smell.

Gawd almighty, your stomach is saying, push on, eh? Your stomach is telling you exactly what to say, now, in Italian. Your stomach demands it, it begs you, it orders *you.*

And the farmer grins and gestures at his farmer's wife, a small woman wrapped in a shawl, with a crooked nose and toothless smile like some awful fairy tale –

But before you can say 'I smell the blood of an Englishman' this old crone, this farmer's hag, is piling mounds of steaming spaghetti into cavernous bowls, and filling bucket-sized mugs of wine, and bringing you a tray of warm – Christ it's warm! – bread and you don't half melt at this gorgeous Italian couple's kindness.

And courage. You understand that too, once you've had your feed, had your fill of this famous Italian cuisine you'd heard about. They're bloody courageous putting you up like this, with the German army all about the place and whatnot. You know what they'll do if they catch you – and you know what they'll do if they find out who's been helping.

There are stories. Villages burned. Farmers' families rounded up and executed. Sanctions, too, on supplies. It's pillaging, really, it is, you think – they just take what they want and if you don't like it, lump it, is the message.

It's brewing up, Tojo says, and something's going to go off, resistance are all at it, and you've heard the Krauts aren't taking any bloody chances.

The partisans are dead men and women.

And the old fella's asking if you're parachutists and Tojo has decided to trust him and that means that you've decided to trust him too. So Tojo tells him you're looking for your mob by the church, and that no one's shown and he says he'll ask around, subtle like, as there's Germans all about the place, he tells you.

And then he takes you to one of the barns, one of the barns filled with straw, and it's bloody luxury, it is, and in moments, you're out like a —

*

Challenor's sitting in the Italian delicatessen on Clerkenwell Road, right by the church. Terroni and Sons, established 1878, so the sign says. There's bloody ham hanging *everywhere*, all about the place, it is. Radio's playing some nonsense about monster mash and a graveyard smash. Gordon Bennett, he's thinking, is this what we've come to? Bloody novelty ghoul music? *Coffin bangers arrive*, he hears. Too bloody right. Coffin for our music scene! Might need a couple, big old hearse, he's thinking —

'Help you?'

Challenor looks up. 'What on earth is this nonsense about monster mash and so on?' he says. He gestures at the room, the sound.

The young woman laughs. 'It's a new hit, they say,' she says. 'You not heard it? Bobby Pickett and the Crypt-Kickers. Just in time for Halloween, innit?'

'Oh yeah? What a name. What a racket.'

The woman tosses him a magazine folded open to the news section. 'Have a look at this if you fancy something less, well, less — '

'Less of a racket?'

'Something like that.'

Challenor examines the magazine. It is the *New Musical Express*. He looks at the cover. September 21, today's date. Well up on the news, then, it must be. His head, well, his head has only gone and *cleared*, he thinks. His head is running smooth. His head's a bloody Rolls-Royce now.

'Can I help you with anything else?' the woman asks.

Challenor's studying the magazine. 'Just a minute,' he says, not looking up.

'I'm going nowhere,' the woman replies.

Challenor reads. There's a story about two 13-year-old schoolgirls called Sue and Mary who are releasing a record on Decca. Fair enough. More bloody novelty. And then he reads about a Liverpool group called The Beatles who have recorded a song called 'Love Me Do' to be released on Parlophone in October.

'You heard of The Rolling Stones?' Challenor asks the woman.

'Oh, yeah,' she says. 'I was there at their first gig, the Marquee, in fact, not long ago. You know them then?'

'Were you now,' Challenor says, thinking of old Wilf. 'I did hear about that gig, in fact, yes. Quite a scene, I've heard.'

'I don't know about scene. Soho, innit?'

Challenor grins. 'I know Soho, girl.'

'So,' the woman asks, and not at all unfriendly, no, absolutely not unfriendly, not at all. 'Anything else I can help you with?'

'Might be, yes,' Challenor says. 'You're not Maria, are you?'

The woman smiles. 'We've all got a Maria in us somewhere.'

Challenor snorts. 'That's very profound.'

The woman laughs. 'No, I mean in our *names*. Though, yeah, profound – very.'

'I'm after the Maria with the Maria at the beginning of her name, I believe. Young Riccardo's cousin.'

The woman gives Challenor a look. She nods. She smiles a wry, but rueful smile, yes *rueful*, Challenor thinks, a rueful smile. But touched with amusement, there's that in it too.

'Maria's in the church next door.'

'Getting some peace and quiet then, is she?'

'Skiving.'

Challenor laughs. Radio's playing old Sherry again. Frankie Valli is a man after my own heart, Challenor thinks.

Challenor says, 'And thanks for the tip.' He gestures again at the room, the sound. 'I'll keep my ears pinned and my eyes peeled.'

The woman smiles a devilish smile. 'Sue and Mary's new disc, you mean?'

'All right, settle down, girl,' Challenor says. He stands. He wriggles into his coat, wraps his scarf. 'I'm going next door for a pray.'

*

There's no sign of any of them at the church. We've been back together and separately now three times, over two days.'

'Yes, sir.'

'The farmer has, he's told me, been making some discreet enquiries, and there has been no word of any other parachutists. No sign at all.'

'Yes, sir.'

'I think it's safe to say, Tanky, that we're extremely unlikely to find our colleagues any time soon.'

'Yes, sir.'

'We've now stayed beyond the time we were instructed by Dudgeon to wait.'

'Yes, sir.'

'And we can't stay here too much longer, if for no other reason than we'll endanger the lives of our generous hosts.'

'We will, sir.'

'It's the moment, Tanky, I think, to call it.'

'Yes, sir.'

'We've got another set of explosives. We can see the Pontremoli-La Spezia line down there below the farmhouse.'

'We can, sir.'

'And the farmer says there are trains running fairy regularly along it.'

'He does, sir.'

'We'll leave at midnight. Lay the charges. Wait for the poor train's whistle, the blast, and we'll scram. We'll head south, during the day, high in the mountains, the spine.'

'Good plan, sir.'

'Head south by the sun, keep to the high ground. Swerve any towns that might be playing host to our German friends.'

'Yes, sir.' You tell yourself: it'll be a cake walk.

'Then it's agreed.'

Yes, sir. And you're pleased –

You're itching to get at it again. Growing fat on pasta and booze is all well and good, and a blessed relief for a day or three, but, you know, you're – what's the word? – you're hungry. *You're hungry to get at it again.*

Bloody glad you didn't have to make the decision, mind.

*

The Italian church has that Roman Catholic nose to it, that Vatican bouquet; the old incense thurible's been shaken around in here not too long ago, Challenor thinks.

Confession dust, it is, the smell of sins old and musty. Challenor smiles. Why he doesn't go to church, on a regular like, on a regular like, *basis.* But he likes the comfort of the scratchy smell of dust and incense, the hang of it in the air, the cloud of it, taking you back to Italy, prompting thoughts of chanting priests and ominous organ notes, of choristers, of old women dressed in black, cackling some intonation or other.

Challenor circles the pews – is it pews? he thinks, in a Roman Catholic set-up, a Roman Catholic *arena*, really – the hard, dark-wooden pews not as comfortable looking as he remembered the opulent seating arrangements in your genuine Italian church, in the churches he popped into in Italy, not all that long ago. They looked a lot easier to park your behind on, those rather more opulent seats, *pews*, or whatever it is the Pope decrees they should be called.

He looks up at the ceiling. It curves, broadly, into a bell shape. There are pale blue squares interrupted by religious artworks, angels flying about the place, men in military tunics collapsing, some half-man/half-wild-eyed-hunchbacked-reptilian-mythological-beast seems to be prowling around, all claws and fangs, terrifying naked children, who are clinging to their naked mothers' breasts. That sort of thing, thinks Challenor. All gold trim and apocalypse and, go on then, son, confess to whatever it is that makes you happy and Bob's your uncle. Just don't call your priest your uncle, Challenor thinks.

Challenor runs a hand over the back of a pew. Wooden, hard, he feels its ridges and lines, its *history*. They've all got it in them, this history. Every church and every pew has got history dripping out of it, pouring out of it, this history is. Challenor wonders about the history of this London Italian church. It's been around the block, after all, hasn't it? It's been around, it's seen things. It's the centre of a little community, after all, to be fair. This church, the poky social club next door, the little delicatessen next to that –

The sort of place you'll find the elder, respectable – or not very respectable, of course – members of this community. And, after all, this centre of the community is not five minutes' walk from Carlo's restaurant on Theobalds Road, outside which young King Oliva was shot, not too long ago.

Challenor's heels click as he approaches the front of the church, heads towards the, you know, what's the word, the *altar*. The *front* is the point. The spot where your chanting, incense-shaking shaman is doing his thing. Got the look of it that you fancy the odd virgin has been sacrificed here, Challenor thinks. Over the years, got to have been one or two virgins given up in a sacrifice for old God. Challenor smiles. *Now* he's being silly.

There's a cough behind him and he turns –

'Help you?'

A young, dark-haired woman who looks really very like the young, dark-haired woman in the delicatessen is standing about halfway down the, well, *aisle*. Roman Catholic or any other persuasion, really, it's still an aisle, isn't it, after all.

'Maria?' Challenor says.

'Yes, I'm Maria.' She pauses. 'One of them, at least.'

'Which one?' Challenor walks towards her and she's walking towards him, and they are destined to meet a few pews back from the front.

'Of the Pedrini Marias,' she says, as they stand facing each other now, squarely, her arms crossed, but smiling, his hands in pockets, an appeasing sort of grin, about two or three feet from each other, they are now, in the aisle, a little distance from the front of this historical Italian church.

'I believe I know the clan,' Challenor says. He grins a little more. He leans against one of the hard, wooden seats, one of the pews, casual like. 'I think you might be able to help me, *cattiva* Maria.'

She raises her eyebrows at that. 'You what?' she says, arms more firmly crossed now. This is not a word she hears that often from an English fella, Challenor suspects, especially not from the gob of some middle-aged, bull-like detective.

'You're friendly with young Joseph Oliva, aren't you?'

Challenor's straight to the point. He's got the right Maria, he knows that, and so he thinks, what's the point buggering about, let's get straight to it, straight to the point.

Maria winces, sneers. 'Who are you, then, grandad, speaking Italian, asking me questions like that?' she says. '*Cattiva?*' she adds. 'Cheeky sod. I should tell my cousin.'

'Riccardo?' Challenor smiles.

Maria looks less than thrilled by all this, Challenor thinks. One more twist, and she's his.

'Yeah,' she says, sulking now. 'What of it?'

'Oh,' says Challenor, 'only that Riccardo and I know each other. Business. We have *business*. You know what I mean?'

It's a question. Challenor waits for an answer –

Maria nods.

'So?' Challenor says. 'My other question.'

Maria nods again. 'Yes,' she says.

'You seeing him tonight?'

Maria nods.

'Good,' Challenor says. 'Good.' He nods to himself and paces a couple of times, takes a turn in between the two sets of pews. 'You here for a pray, are you?' he says.

This throws young Maria a little, Challenor sees. Challenor sits down. He *takes a pew*. He gestures for young Maria to do the same. She shakes her head. She wraps her arms a touch more tightly around her chest.

'Well?' Challenor says.

'I work next door,' Maria says. 'Sometimes I help out here with the books.' She nods towards the back of the church. 'In the office.'

'Anyone else there?'

'Nah, just me today.'

'Not skiving then?'

Maria frowns, but there is a hint, Challenor thinks, a *hint* of a smile behind it. 'Who you been talking to?' she says.

Challenor grins. 'None of your beeswax, girl.' He jogs his knees in the cold. They're always *cold*, churches, he thinks.

'So,' Maria asks. 'You mind telling me who you are?'

'You work for old Wilf Gardiner, I've heard.'

'Worked. Past tense. You didn't answer my question.'

Challenor pulls his credentials. 'Detective Sergeant Challenor, West End Central. That's Soho to you, love.'

Maria is nodding now, she's nodding and she's looking a touch, well, more than a touch, nervous.

Challenor goes on. 'So you used to work at Gardiner's place, and now you don't, and your cousin and your fella and Gardiner have fallen out. That about right?'

Maria nods.

Challenor goes on. 'So you're going to do me a little favour today, right? What you're going to do, girl, is you're going to go and tell your cousin and your fella that Detective Sergeant Challenor came to see you and that he said that if this business with old Wilf Gardiner is not sorted out *right now* then he's going to bring you in on a solicitation charge. You know what that is?'

Maria shakes her head.

Challenor goes on. 'Well, Maria, you're well aware of what goes on in old Wilf Gardiner's nightclubs, aren't you?' She nods. 'So you'll also know that there are ways for his employees – his *female* employees – to make a little extra money, upstairs, with the customers.' She nods again. 'And you'll also know that for one of these female employees to offer this service is strictly against the law.' She nods again. 'Well, love, it's not going to be too hard for me to find someone who will testify that you did just that in your time as a female employee of Wilf Gardiner's cabaret and revue bar, to give it its full name. *Capisci?*'

Maria nods. 'I understand,' she says. 'Today, right?'

'As soon as, my girl.'

Maria's nodding. 'And that's all? I pass on this message, and...'

'And we're rosy, love. *You*, my dear, have nothing to worry about.' Challenor pauses. 'I'm not interested in you,' he says.

Challenor stands. He bows, half to young Maria, half to the church –

Challenor clicks off up the aisle, through the heavy wooden door, down the steps, two at a time, and into a fresh little early-autumn morning –

With a fat, mischievous grin plastered right across his mug.

*

It's the eighteenth of September, eleven days after you were dropped down, down in the dark, the dark, cool night, noiselessly, floating noiselessly down through that immense, deep blue-black night, down into – onto – Italy –

Italy.

You're full of pasta and wine and coffee and bread and butter and sausage and ham and you're hungry –

The farmer's wife has filled a bag for you, filled it with bread and ham and sausage and wine, and you hump the bag onto your back, and you heft this huge bag along with the rest of your kit and you walk away from the farmhouse and head straight down the hill and into the trees so that you don't have to turn around and wave – again – goodbye to your kind hosts, your benevolent, understanding, courageous hosts.

Neither of you talk. You're not normally so quiet on the run-up to a job. You're not sure what it is. You think it might be the act of leaving, of, in your mind, abandoning *your colleagues. Of leaving, of abandoning, of* leaving *Dudgeon, Foster, Shortall, Pinckney and Greville-Bell.*

Leaving them behind.

Tojo, you have to assume, is feeling something similar, something familiar, something worse, you, in fairness, have to assume. As you know bloody well that that was not a decision you wanted to take.

So you're saying nothing –

If Tojo wants to talk, you'll talk, but until that moment definitively arises, you're saying nothing.

The trees seem to bend away from you, curve away from you, arch up into the hill and down the other side. White oak, green oak, coni-fers – your basic Italian trees. That's what Tojo's told you, after he's had a parlay with the farmer and learnt a little more about the lay of the land, and not just about Jerry's whereabouts.

The Pontremoli-La Spezia line runs between two hills not a half-day's trudge from the farmhouse. You clock the entrance to a tunnel from the mouth of which an apparently working railway line sticks out, like a metal tongue, and curves and bends away into the valley and through the Apennine mountains.

You wait an hour. You wait and watch the tunnel for an hour –

Then you scramble down using the clusters of basic Italian trees as cover and lay the charges on either side of the single line.

You have no idea how much time you have before a train so you scarper –

You scramble back up the hill and pick up your gear, and your bag of ham and sausage and bread and wine, and you're on your way –

You only reach the foothills though, and there it is: the whistle of a train.

You both pause, stop, cock your ears.

Cock your ears? No need for that:

An ear-drum shattering explosion rings out, echoes out, rolls out between the hills, throbs and hums down the valley –

And you're laughing, both of you are laughing, grinning and laughing, and you calm down and you shake hands and you head south –

South, south towards the Allied lines –

You make south by the sun and you keep to the high ground.

At least that's where you believe they are, these Allied lines.

South.

Easy.

*

Challenor sits at his desk with his head eased, and his head has really dropped a gear in terms of its engine growl, its gorgeous, low, healthy sounding rattle –

It's really humming, now, it is, his head. It's opened up its throttle and is *cruising*, now, it is, his head.

And nobody seems to be too concerned with his little small-hours visit to the cells, and he's thinking about what to do in terms of the evening ahead, and, specifically, he's looking at a list of names and working out which of this list is going to be keeping an eye on the Phoenix tonight, and he works it out, and he wonders.

He wonders what to do.

He's got two options, he reckons –

The first is to tell Police Constable John Bryan Legge and Police Constable Alan David Wells exactly what it is that he suspects will occur this evening around the Phoenix club. He could do that as Legge and Wells are the two aides to CID working that evening and they will be posted at the Phoenix, the eyes and ears for CID.

The second option is to *not* tell Legge and Wells exactly what it is that he suspects will occur this evening around the Phoenix club. He'll do *that*, as although they are the two aides to CID working that evening and will be posted at the Phoenix, the eyes and ears for CID, Challenor does not know these two lads. In fact, these two lads have been attached to West End Central for less than a week, and have had no dealings with Challenor. Challenor's not even sure he's met them.

So, he wonders –

He wonders what to do.

*

'Who dares, eh, Tanky? Three sets of explosives, three trains.'
  Tojo speaks. Finally.

'Who dares, sir. Quite right.'

Tojo nods. He's leading the way along a pretty little ridge, and it really feels like you might be the only two people in the world right now, it does –

'We're OK for food and drink for a few days but it'll be worth figuring a friendly village or, better still, a friendly farm where we can stop to stock up,' Tojo says. 'There's the operational float, so we can offer something for it.'

'You didn't give any to the last lot?' you say.

'I tried to,' Tojo says.

You nod. You're not surprised.

'Sir,' you say.

'Yes, Tanky.'

'How about we, well, how about we spend a little of that float on a, well, you know, on a drink or two.'

Tojo keeps walking, keeps scanning left and right. You're travelling during the day in the higher ground which seems safe, but you never do know, after all, do you?

'You want us to have a drink-up, Tanky?'

'Well – '

'As a celebration, a job well done, do you mean?'

'I – '

'Is there anything else you fancy?'

You think, fuck it, why not. 'Well, sir, we could always look for a bit of the other too, couldn't we?'

Tojo laughs. Tojo stops teasing you. He calls out over his shoulder, 'I don't think you need my help for that, Tanky.'

You smile. To be fair, all you really want is to wake up without any danger of finding yourself peering down the barrel of a rifle.

*

Challenor decides that he's not going to tell Police Constable John Bryan Legge and Police Constable Alan David Wells exactly what it is that he suspects will occur this evening around the Phoenix club.

Let's let this unfold natural like, Challenor thinks.

Yes, that's the badger. He'll sit tight and, you know, what's the word, he'll pull strings, he'll *orchestrate*. He'll puppet-show the whole business.

Yeah, he thinks, I'm not going to tell Legge and Wells exactly what it is that I suspect will occur this evening around the Phoenix club, at a little after 11 p.m. Before midnight, certainly.

Challenor thinks it best he's behind the scenes on this one.

What are you going to do about it?

*

You walk and you walk, you trudge and you hike, you march and you march –

You follow the sun, you keep to the high ground.

Two days of this and your bag of ham and sausage and bread and wine is almost empty.

You look at maps and you look at landmarks and you reckon you're more or less slap bang in the middle of a rough square formed by Villafranca, Bologna, Pisa and Florence.

You spot a village down on the western side of the Apennines. You swoop high around it, hoping to find a quiet farm outside.

You're not sure of the date, you've no idea of the day, and you'll take your chance. This, you understand, is gruelling. You understand this word, now.

You head up the track to the farm and are confronted by a huge, ter-rifying dog, all lethal-looking yellow teeth, all snarl, all snap. The sort of dog who'd chew his own leg off if he's hungry enough.

Your hand drifts to your Schmeisser –

That dog ain't going to take you by the throat, oh no it bloody ain't. You're well aware of your own jugular, and you're hanging on to it, thank you very much.

Tojo has his hands out front, keeping the dog – and you – calm, it appears.

You're frozen, the pair of you, and the dog doesn't seem to want to actually get stuck in. What now?

Then, a broad-hipped woman, thirtyish, dark hair, tasty-looking, calls off the dog. She's flanked by a couple of hefty farmhands.

'Tedesci?' She asks. German?

Tojo shakes his head. 'Inglesi.'

She nods. She comes closer. She has beautiful eyes.

She leads you to a barn filled with hay bales. She and Tojo have a long and faltering conversation. Her husband was in the Italian army and died in the Western Desert. She runs the farm with her two lads. She hates Germans.

She leaves you and you get comfortable and then she's back with plates of pasta and sausage and bread and ham, and wine, lots of wine.

As she refills your glass, you say, 'Belli occhi.' Beautiful eyes. You've learned something. Actually, you've learned a couple of things, the way she takes the compliment.

She clears your plates and glasses.

Tojo stretches out and falls asleep after the meal.

You sit outside the barn, cleaning your guns –

There she is. You wave. She waves. You walk down towards her.

It's dusk. The sky bleeds orange-red. The crisp autumn air snaps as the sun goes down.

'Cattiva Maria.'

Naughty Maria, you're saying, and then you're on the ground and you've her in your hands above you, and she has you in hers, and you're kissing and she rolls off and under you and the warmth and the hunger and the sheer bloody wonder and the out-and-out relief, pleasure, sensation of this moment –

In the dark you walk her back and then you return to the barn and Tojo wakes up and asks where the bloody hell you've been and you tell him you thought you heard something, and he says is everything all right and you say yes, sir, everything seems to be in order, couldn't be better, you say.

And you're bloody well right about that.

Tanky

A few years after my grandad passed on, I started to understand the magnitude of what he'd done – what they'd done. I'd look at a blue photo album he put together. It records their days training in Scotland, blowing up road blocks in France, helping liberate Norway, passing through the rubble of Hamburg in 1945, and the lazy days immediately after: swimming, sunbathing, these impossibly young-looking, fit-looking, relaxed-looking lads. Every time I look at this blue photo album, I well up a touch, have a bit of a cry. Sometimes it's about knowing how much older I am now than they were then. I've never really understood why I feel it, but there's an inadequacy that pops up too, as if how dare I have any problems in the face of what they did. But I know my grandad wouldn't wish some of what he saw, and did, on his worst enemy – on his actual enemy, in fact – that he'd do anything for me and my brother never to have to do what he did.

He always said that SAS was knowing the Germans were there – and knowing they didn't know you were. That was the advantage of being elite. Makes sense.

In that blue photo album, there's a snap of two young, muscular fellas holding up a Nazi flag, looking at it quizzically, both got Woodbines in their gobs. It's in Hamburg. There are ruins all around them.

They're standing in front of a jeep, and on the front of the jeep's spare tyre which sits on the grill in front of the engine, is painted, in white, the words:

Little Tanky

The lad on the right is grinning, his beret at a jaunty angle, I suppose is how you'd describe it. His short sleeves are rolled up, better to accentuate his biceps, his forearms. The lad to the left is dressed more neatly, hand on hip, proudly bearing this Nazi flag. My grandad has written their names under the photo:

Cas Carpenter and Tanky Challenor

There's a bunch of photos of lads lounging around in jeeps in Hamburg, mocking the flags they've pilfered, or examining them, or simply indifferent to them, the flags just there, in the shot, barely noticeable, and the lads are simply enjoying a rest and a smoke. Each photo is inscribed:

Freddie Baines and Will Fyffe
Pouch Maybury and 'Umbriago'
Larry Brownlee and Paddy McCann
Sammy Harrison and Jake Manders
Cas Carpenter and Tanky Challenor

My eye always strays to the photo of Tanky – the lunatic looks about twelve years old. And there he is, with his jeep, his pride and joy: Little Tanky.

Four

'It's that bastard Gardiner; he's grassed on us. It's a nice club he's got. If he charges me, he won't have it for long.'

Challenor's marching down the corridors of West End Central, the Mad House, he's really marching, stamping, he is, *stampeding* down the corridors of the nick, *his* nick, *his* Mad House, his boots clicking and thumping as he marches, as he stamps –

And he's wearing a grin bigger than a soldier's in a Mediterranean bordello, two days into leave.

It has all, he is very happy to admit, gone according to plan. It has all gone exactly according plan. Clockwork, it's gone, bloody smooth as. Smooth as bloody Yank silk stockings, it's gone, and Challenor is having his little pace around his nick to calm down a touch, to get his bonce straight and his mug right as they've got Riccardo Pedrini and Alan Cheeseman in the cells downstairs and Challenor is very keen, eager he is, *itching* to have a word with these two and start wrapping up this little nonsense once and for all.

Wells and Legge have got Cheeseman and Pedrini downstairs and Challenor's plan has gone very well indeed. It was, he reflects, quite a good idea not to tell these young police constables exactly what it was that he suspected would occur earlier this evening around the Phoenix club. Now, he hopes, the next stage of his plan will unfold with quite the same symmetry and inevitability.

Inevitable, yes, he thinks, that's what it was –

Inevitable.

Better inevitable than predictable, that's for sure. Something old Tojo used to say, something old Tojo referred to once in terms of *narrative*, in terms of plot, that it was better for something to be inevitable than predictable. Course, he was comparing their Italian exploits to the workings of a novel, a thriller, but Challenor reckons the comparison stands its ground, is fair enough.

Good old Tojo.

Challenor reaches the cells. The charge room is empty now. On the table –

Cheeseman's possessions and Pedrini's possessions –

Challenor examines them. He examines the document that records the confiscation of the possessions of arrested men, a list. It's unsigned. Challenor's not sure. He thinks for a moment. He's not messing about, Challenor, and he knows what to do.

He knows.

Challenor barrels down the corridor, either side of which are the cells, the famous Mad House cells. Most of these famous Mad House cells are empty, he notices. Two of them, down at the end of this corridor, are showing No Vacancies, Challenor can see by the red lights on above the doors.

Outside these two cells are Police Constable John Bryan Legge and Police Constable Alan David Wells.

Challenor decides that he'll talk to Wells.

'Wells,' he barks. 'With me.'

Challenor turns on his heel. Challenor spins, windmills around, doesn't stop for a second, he windmills around, he does, with no loss of momentum and storms off back towards the charge room. He doesn't look back or wait for Police Constable Alan David Wells, but he can feel him there behind him, trying to keep up, trying and failing to keep up with Challenor's bustle, his head-down charge for the charge room, a bull with a tense neck and a serious face on for a herd.

Challenor throws open the door of the charge room and turns to face his aide. He looks at the table which holds the possessions of the two arrested men. He looks at Police Constable Alan David Wells.

'Wells,' he says. 'Cheeseman's?'

Wells indicates.

'Right,' Challenor says. 'And he admitted to this, did he?' Challenor's pointing at a flick knife.

Wells looks unsure for a moment. Wells's eyes flash doubt, just for a second.

'Well, Wells?' Challenor says, with a smirk.

Wells nods, nods furiously. 'Yes, sir.'

'And these are Pedrini's?' Challenor asks, pointing at the other collection of possessions.

Wells is sure of this, and confident now, he is, onto a winner here, he feels. 'Yes, sir,' he says, emphatically.

'And this,' Challenor says, picking up a piece of iron tubing, 'he admitted to this, did he?'

Wells looks unsure again. 'I might need to ask – '

Challenor raises his eyebrows.

Wells shakes his head. 'No, I mean, yes, sir, yes, those are all Pedrini's possessions.'

Challenor's nodding. 'Sign here,' he says, pointing at the document on the table that records the confiscation of the possessions of arrested men.

Wells has learnt something here, and he doesn't hesitate, signs with a flourish, in fact, Challenor spots. Quite a flourish, he's got, young Wells, with that pen there.

'Thank you, Wells,' Challenor says. 'You can jog on, now.' Challenor smiles. 'As you were. Send Legge down here to see me, if you will.'

'Yes, sir,' Wells says.

Challenor waits. Challenor stands and waits, nodding, grinning, tapping his foot. One quick word here with young Police Constable John Bryan Legge and Bob's your uncle and all that jazz, and here we fucking go –

'Sir?' Legge's head is in the doorway.

'Come in, come in,' Challenor says, shooing him in the door.

Legge stands straight and tall.

Challenor is waving the document that Wells has recently signed with such a flourish. 'Check this please, Legge,' he says.

Legge takes a look at the document. Legge reads the list of possessions, scans the list, scans it quite carefully, Challenor reckons, and his face changes, a touch, not more than a flicker, as he reads it, but it definitely changes, once or twice. Legge looks at the table. Legge looks back at the list. Legge looks at the table again, and then, again, he looks back at the list, he *studies* the list.

'Well?' Challenor asks, all friendly now, *helpful*. 'All look about right?'

Legge is nodding. 'Yes, sir. It does.'

Challenor smiles. 'Good lad,' he says. 'Countersign, would you?'

Legge countersigns and leaves, sharpish.

Challenor smiles. Challenor *grins*.

*

'So what you're telling me, Tanky,' Tojo is saying, over a coffee and a smoke the morning after, 'is that you've gone and bedded our hostess within about an hour of us pitching up, as it were.'

You both chuckle.

'Yes, sir, I suppose so,' you say. 'Not sure "bedding" is quite the right term, though.'

'I didn't take you for a pedantic one, Tanks.'

'Eh, sir?'

'Nothing, nothing.' Tojo smokes. Tojo smirks. 'I suppose it was inevitable.'

'Inevitable, sir?'

'She's a widower, her husband's death Jerry's fault, we're here to rescue her, effectively, and you're a likely looking young buck.' He smiles. 'Yeah,' he says. 'Inevitable. Or predictable.'

'What's the difference?' you ask.

Tojo laughs. 'If it's inevitable, it's heroic.' He pauses, nods, he likes that, does Tojo. 'And if it's predictable, it's cheap. Yeah. That's the difference.'

Good old Tojo.

'Definitely inevitable then, sir,' you say.

And the pair of you have a good laugh –

And it's about bloody time, you think.

*

Cheeseman first.

Challenor stomps down the corridor, the corridor lined with empty cells, stomping, snorting, smashing his way down this corridor to the two cells that have red lights on above their doors –

He points at the door to one of these cells and Police Constable John Bryan Legge takes a fat bunch of keys and opens the door.

Challenor doesn't so much enter the cell as invade it. It must feel, to its occupant, that Challenor has had to narrow his considerable frame to fit through the cell door, that he may, in fact, have had to smash his way in *sideways*. The cell, with Challenor in it, suddenly feels especially inadequate. *There is not enough cell* is the impression that Challenor aims for when he inflicts himself on this, or any other, tiny, inadequate cell.

'Cheeseman,' he says. 'You know who I am.'

Cheeseman nods.

Challenor says, 'We'll be charging you with possession, at least. You might as well get used to that.'

'Possession of what?'

Challenor smiles. Poor young lad. How old is Cheeseman? About twenty?

'Don't take the mickey,' Challenor says, 'you'll only get me angry.'

Challenor steps further into the cell and slaps Cheeseman, hard, open-handed, and then again, also hard, this time back-handed.

Cheeseman recoils, bends over. It's the shock as much as the pain, Challenor thinks of telling him. He doesn't tell him. Instead, he lifts Cheeseman's head by the hair. He pulls Cheeseman's not unattractive face towards his own. Cheeseman's not unattractive face is reddening on both sides. Is going quite puce, Challenor sees.

Challenor pulls the flick knife that was not long before on the table in the charge room. He opens this flick knife.

In one hand he holds Cheeseman's head, looks into the eyes of his not unattractive face; in the other hand, he holds Cheeseman's flick knife, Cheeseman's open flick knife. The knife is not a considerable distance from Cheeseman's throat.

'I believe this is yours,' Challenor says.

Cheeseman shakes his head.

Challenor breathes. Well, he snorts, really. He lets out a long breath, and its ferocity make a sort of snort, a growl.

'You are a known associate of Joseph Oliva,' Challenor says.

Cheeseman shakes his head.

Challenor smiles. There is a nasty edge to this smile. He turns the knife about in his hand and thinks about what to do with it.

'You and Pedrini and Oliva and your associates have been demanding money with menaces,' Challenor says.

Cheeseman shakes his head.

Challenor folds the flick knife and pockets it. Then, holding Cheeseman's hair, he drags him across the cell. Well, the cell being a cell, what he really does here is *yank* Cheeseman two steps over to a chair. He pulls Cheeseman, using his hair as a lever, onto this chair.

Cheeseman sits and is looking pretty glum, Challenor thinks. His lip is thickening up something nice, and his hair, now that Challenor has let it go, is all over the place.

'That's what happens when you use so much Brylcreem,' Challenor says.

'What's that then?' Cheeseman stutters.

'Your mess of a mop, son. It'll hold its shape, I suspect. You look like a shrub, my young beauty.'

Cheeseman says nothing to this. Challenor wonders if Cheeseman might cry. He wonders if he *should* cry, if he should make Cheeseman cry.

Challenor grabs Cheeseman by the jaw. He squeezes, hard. He twists Cheeseman's head by his jaw, like he's screwing Cheeseman's head onto a spike and he's using the jaw as leverage – first the hair as a lever, now the jaw – using the jaw as a means of really making sure this head is secure on its spike, properly screwed on and secure. There is no way Cheeseman's head is going anywhere.

'Right then,' Challenor says. 'You've got the gist. You know why you're here. If you're in possession of the fact, I suggest you air your knowledge, chum.'

Challenor releases Cheeseman's jaw. Challenor slaps Cheeseman, open hand, lightly, twice. Challenor ruffles Cheeseman's hair, pinches his cheek.

'Don't go to sleep, my old darling,' he says. 'I'm coming back.'

*

You sit down with hot goat's milk, bread and figs –

Italian peasant farmer's breakfast.

Maria is all smiles. Tojo is quietly shaking his head and smiling. You haven't felt better in what feels like an age. A soldier's life! You're thinking –

Full belly, the love of a good woman, a red wine slumber and a decent breakfast buffet. What more can any man ask for!

Well, safe passage, that's the next thing Tojo is thinking about –

The route to safety.

Maria has brought her brother to breakfast and Tojo's chatting to him about the mountain route, the trek you're about to continue, and you're making eyes at Maria and thinking that maybe you could just stay, melt into the background and stay and forget all about this war and these decisions you've made that have meant you've ended up here, hiding, fleeing now –

And then Tojo says, 'Let's go, Tanks. The path's clear for miles.' He nods at Maria's brother. 'He's been asking around. We need to get a wriggle on while it's safe.'

You nod. You grunt and you nod and you bid them a fond farewell and hit the track, your boots into that old groove, that march, that stomp, that trudge –

One foot in front of the other, your hand on your Schmeisser and your eyes peeled –

Seconds, minutes, hours.

*

Challenor storms across the corridor and steams into Pedrini's cell –

Pedrini's sitting on the chair in the corner of the cell. His jacket is hung neatly on the back of the chair. He is leaning forward with his elbows on his knees. He is smoking a cigarette. His top button has been opened and his tie loosened. His hair is a hardening oil-slick of grease. It looks like you could snap it, his hair. He is clean-shaven. His shirt is crisp white, recently ironed. The sleeves are rolled up. His shoes are in the Yank style, two-tone brogues, polished right up.

Challenor takes all this in and thinks to himself that he's going to enjoy this, that young Pedrini here probably needn't have got so dressed up, that perhaps the lad might think twice next time he rolls in here with quite such a cocky, sneering, superior, jungle-cat disposition.

'Up,' Challenor says.

Pedrini smiles. Slowly – slowly – he pushes the chair back and stands. He takes the cigarette from his mouth and drops it theatrically to the floor. He then rolls his shirtsleeves down. He buttons them up. He then does up the top button of his shirt and adjusts his tie. He takes the jacket from the back of the chair and puts it on. He pushes his wrists through to the end and makes sure that his cuffs are lined up as they should be, almost the exact same amount of white peeking from this slick, well-cut, navy blue Italian suit he's wearing.

All this takes some time. And times stretches in the pressure cooker of a cell when that cell is currently shared with Detective Sergeant Harold Challenor. Which is to say that the short time it takes for Pedrini to go through this little routine is a very long time indeed.

Challenor applauds, ironically.

'You cut quite a dash,' Challenor says. 'You know, for a prisoner.'

Pedrini says nothing.

Challenor takes the piece of iron tubing from his inside pocket; the same iron tubing that was not long ago on the table in the charge room.

'This is yours,' Challenor says.

Pedrini nods. Challenor raises his eyebrows.

Pedrini nods and smiles. 'It's my cigar holder,' Pedrini says.

Challenor is nodding now. He tosses it in his right hand. He spins it and catches it.

He's nodding.

'Let me get this straight,' Challenor says.

With his left hand he grabs Pedrini's lapel. He yanks him three feet across the cell, hard, so that Pedrini bangs his shoulder against the wall. Challenor, using only his left hand and forearm, muscles Pedrini into a corner of the cell. He takes his hand off Pedrini's lapel and, in quick succession, punches Pedrini, hard, in the stomach, then, as Pedrini doubles over, grabs his head by the hair and pushes it up against the wall. He lifts Pedrini's head as high as Pedrini's neck will allow.

Pedrini is breathing very heavily.

'Let me get this straight,' Challenor says.

He takes the piece of iron tubing and fixes the opening at one end over Pedrini's left eye, so that it forms a sort of child's pretend telescope.

He pushes it over Pedrini's eye very firmly so that it will mark, it will *bruise*, quite dramatically, Pedrini's eye socket.

'Let me get this straight,' Challenor says. 'If this is your cigar holder, my darling,' he grinds the tubing with greater ferocity and blood starts to drip then trickle then fall from the vicinity of Pedrini's left eye, 'if this is your cigar holder, then,' he takes it from Pedrini's eye and examines it himself, looks through it, 'if this is your cigar holder, young man, then where the fuck is your cigar!'

Challenor takes one final look at the tubing. He spins it in his hand then pokes it very firmly indeed into Pedrini's stomach. Pedrini doubles up again – he gasps and is clearly in considerable pain, Challenor can see that – and Challenor has a firm grip with his left hand around Pedrini's throat.

'You offered Police Constable Alan David Wells a hundred pounds if he'd see you all right,' Challenor says.

Pedrini says nothing. Challenor slaps Pedrini's face with his right hand.

'You are a known associate of Joseph Oliva and the two of you, with others, are involved in a protection racket in Soho and parts of Camden.'

Pedrini says nothing. Challenor slaps Pedrini's face with his right hand.

'Johnnie Ford ran off tonight when you were approached and was then apprehended by Police Constable Alan David Wells and Police Constable John Bryan Legge.'

Pedrini says nothing. Challenor does nothing.

'Where the fuck's Johnnie Ford?'

Pedrini says nothing. Challenor slaps Pedrini's face with his right hand.

'Where the fuck's Johnnie Ford?'

Pedrini says nothing. Challenor slaps Pedrini's face with his right hand.

'Where the fuck's Johnnie Ford?'

Pedrini says nothing. Challenor slaps Pedrini's face with his right hand.

Challenor pulls Pedrini by the throat across the cell. Pedrini is bleeding quite heavily now, around the left eye, and in and around his puffed-up mouth, his swollen mouth, which, Challenor notes, is not doing much other than bleeding.

He plonks Pedrini down on the chair. He pulls the chair and Pedrini into the middle of the cell. He takes Pedrini's tie and undoes it. He holds Pedrini's tie in both hands, and turns it a couple of times around each of his palms so that he is now holding it very securely indeed. He moves behind Pedrini and places the tie around his neck.

He pulls the tie, hard, and tightens it around Pedrini's neck, like a garrotte.

Pedrini's hands go to his neck. Hopeless.

He gasps and gags and coughs and hacks and tries to scream out, to shout –

Challenor holds firm, keeps his grip secure.

Challenor keeps this up for a short time, but in the cell it feels like a very long time indeed.

He comes round to face Pedrini, the tie still in his hand. Pedrini is dazed. Pedrini closes his eyes, rolls his head. His neck has gone. He is rolling his head partly because his neck has gone and partly because he is trying to avoid Challenor.

Challenor grabs Pedrini by the jaw. Pedrini's jaw is already dis-colouring, Challenor sees.

He says, meaning the tie, 'I'll take this. Suicide watch.'

Pedrini groans.

'You know where we are now, champ. I'll see you soon.'

Challenor raps on the door with his knuckles. Police Constable Alan David Wells opens the cell door. Police Constable Alan David Wells knows better than to look past Challenor and inside the cell. Challenor notes this, pleased.

He stalks off down the corridor, the corridor lined with empty cells –

Nearly there, he thinks.

What are you going to do about it?

Go on, my son.

*

You walk. You keep to the high ground. The sun is high, autumn fresh, air crisp. It's not so different, you think, to parts of Scotland, near Inverness, where you trained not such a long time ago.

The same but different. The colours are the same but not quite. The trees are the same but not quite. The rocks on the ground, the stones, they're the same but they're not. Everything feels slightly off, slightly out of focus, the colours dampened, filtered somehow so that you recognise them, you know what they are, but they are unmistakably Italian and not English, Scottish, British.

On a sunny day, the light is almost unbearable to look at –

This is a relief.

You can pretend you're not there. If you can't really see where you are, you're not really there. And the seconds bleed into the minutes bleed into the hours bleed into the days, the days –

You barely speak. Tojo's feet are swollen. Your feet are swollen. Your rations are running very low. The top boys had no idea you'd be gone this long.

But the sun is high and the high ground is safe and there are ways, there are always ways for men like you to get what you need.

And then in what feels like a hallucination, a very old Italian man is pouring olive oil on a bed of frying weeds or grass and you're eating and it's delicious and the old man's goats are scrawny, but they're there so there is milk but no wine –

The old man is very apologetic regarding the lack of wine.

Tojo peels off some notes, a bundle of lira.

'Time for a drink, Tanky,' he says.

*

'Right,' Challenor says to Police Constable John Bryan Legge and Police Constable Alan David Wells. 'Your versions, please.'

The two police constables look at each other. Challenor's got short odds on Legge to talk first.

Legge says, 'Well, sir, we located the group under surveillance leaving the Lorraine club in Soho. There was a number of young women with them. At least two of these young women peeled off and did not join the rest of the group on the way to the Phoenix.'

Challenor smiles. 'Did anyone keep an eye on these two women?'

'No,' Legge says. 'We understood that we were to keep with the group under suspicion.'

'Quite right,' Challenor says. He is thinking about Josephine Jennings and cousin Maria Pedrini. 'Do go on.'

'Some others in the group dispersed, but we stuck with Pedrini and Cheeseman and one other man who we believe to be Johnnie Ford.'

'You stuck with those three?'

'They were making for the Phoenix club with considerable purpose, was our interpretation of the situation.'

'You did the right thing. Go on.'

'When they arrived at the door of the Phoenix,' Legge is saying, 'the proprietor, Wilf Gardiner, was standing outside with a large man having a cigarette. The two men seemed relaxed, and Gardiner was telling a joke or story, and the large man – an employee, we believe – was laughing politely. The three men we were observing went straight over to Gardiner and began haranguing him. Gardiner's employee stood firm but was given strict instructions by Gardiner not to intervene.'

'OK,' Challenor says. 'What was said?'

Legge continues, 'We weren't able to follow every word of the altercation, but a sum of money – a hundred pounds – was certainly referred to, as well as a number of threats. At one point we believe we heard Pedrini say to Ford "come on, let's do him up, let's stripe the bastard. The aggro he's given us". There was a moment then that the two groups of men came together, briefly, yes, there was a definite physical exchange. It was at this point we made ourselves known.'

Challenor is smiling. 'And after you'd made yourselves known?'

'As we crossed the road, Gardiner clocked us and said something like "about bloody time" which spooked the three lads and one of them, Ford, as I said, we believe it was Ford, scarpered. Seeing it was only two of us on the scene, we let him go. We figured we could find him later and do him for resisted as well as anything else.'

'Good thinking,' Challenor says, grinning. He taps the side of his head and looks at his two police constables. 'Not just a hat rack, eh, lads?' he says. 'Do go on.'

'We held the four men, who have by this time calmed down, and waited for the police van which arrived minutes later. As we're waiting, Gardiner says something like "I'm fucking bleeding here, officers, the fucking wop bastards have nicked me, they've cut me" and we can confirm that his ear was bleeding, though the nature of the cut was far from fatal, if you get my drift.'

Challenor certainly does get Police Constable John Bryan Legge's drift. He grins – *wide*.

'Good old Wilf,' Challenor says, the irony rather more obvious than old Wilf's wound. 'And Gardiner gave a witness statement, and you charged Cheeseman and Pedrini, and now here we all are?'

Police Constable John Bryan Legge and Police Constable Alan David Wells both nod.

Challenor nods.

This is all going *exactly* according to plan.

*

You dig around in your pockets. You throw a few more notes at the old man –

'You better take a barrow,' you say.

Tojo laughs and translates.

You sit and you wait for three long hours. You don't know this very old man from Adam. But for the previous two nights – like scores of others previous – you have slept in a bush, cuddling together to repel the cold, and the strain of this discomfort, the physical toll it's taken, coupled with the fear of getting caught, of being betrayed or captured, has meant Tojo will take a risk on this very old Italian man.

You sit stock still, not expending any energy. This is how you were trained. Whenever you get a chance to rest, whenever there is any down time at all, take it, shut down, recharge, try out a bit of the old Italian chit chat with Tojo.

You take half-hour shifts and get a little shut-eye and rest your legs and your feet. Your feet. Christ. All four of them are blue, peeling, blisters taking hold all over them, your feet more blister than foot, to be fair.

Tojo's are worse. Quite a lot worse. You say nothing. It's the senior officer's prerogative to comment on, or not comment on, any physical issues he may, or may not, be having. You keep your trap shut, you keep your, what's the word, your counsel.

The very old Italian man returns with more wine than you can shake a goat herder's staff at. And seeing as the very old man is a goat herder and has a goat herder's staff, you are able to prove this hypothesis, you are able to prove it quite a number of times, and it's especially funny to demonstrate this proof after a good deal of the wine has been sunk.

Good, solid drinking, you have. It's got a hell of a thump to it, your Italian peasant wine. And with little to eat for days but raw chestnuts, it certainly hefts you along with it, certainly pummels you into quick submission.

You remember:

Trying to sing a dirty song under a star-filled sky on the high ground of the Apennines, and directing this song at the sophisticated folks of Florence, who are, you reckon, not too many miles away.

You remember:

Not getting much of an audience for this dirty ditty, this drunken chorister's performance, as your very old Italian host is fast asleep with his head on your makeshift table, and Lieutenant Wedderburn is occupied with giving the old coot something of a stern lecture on the essentials of mountaineering.

*

Challenor's back in the charge room and this time he is with Johnnie Ford.

It is now 1.30 in the morning. Approximately half an hour earlier, Challenor is told, Police Constables David Leonard Harris and David Paul Stephenson picked up Johnnie Ford. When Johnnie Ford was told that he was being arrested for demanding money with menaces, he is alleged to have said: 'It's that bastard Gardiner; he's grassed on us. It's a nice club he's got. If he puts the needle to me, he won't have it for long.'

On arrival at West End Central, Johnnie Ford was searched but nothing of any consequence was found on his person.

Challenor and Ford are sitting in the charge room and Challenor is calm. Ford, however, is agitated, perhaps understandably, given his recent arrest. Challenor's calm is intended as a riposte to Ford's agitation, and designed by Challenor to wind Ford up further. Challenor knows that Ford has a temper and that Ford has a history of violent behaviour and Challenor reckons the opposite approach to that which he took with Cheeseman and Pedrini is the way to go.

Ford is jiggling his knee and smoking furiously and Challenor is calmly taking down his antecedents. Challenor is not engaging with Ford one bit and Ford is not enjoying this.

'Can I speak to you, guv?' Ford says.

Challenor looks up from his paperwork and smiles. 'Nothing would make me happier, Jonathan. It is Jonathan, is it not?'

'I – '

'And let's not forget that you're still under caution here. I wouldn't say or do anything, and so on, as you well know.'

'That's all right,' Ford says. 'I'm knackered anyway, but don't get the wrong idea. This is all a take-on, know what I mean? A mickey-take, that's all it is, a leg-pull. Joe Oliva and a few of the boys have been taking the piss out of him, out of Gardiner, that's all it is. He's a ponce, and we're mucking about, that's all. We wouldn't have had his money, it was just frighteners. That's all it was, frighteners.'

Challenor smiles. 'Frighteners?'

'Yeah, just frighteners, straight up.'

'Either way,' Challenor says. 'I'll show you to your room.'

＊

Your head thrums. Your head zips. Your head zings. Your head –

Your head is in a bloody right old state when you wake up. Tojo doesn't look too clever either, but your very old Italian peasant goat herder friend is up with the chickens, as they say, and humming a tune – some bloody opera, you expect – and preparing you a breakfast of goat's milk and chestnut bread.

You wolf down this breakfast, and then have a second go, and a third, and your host is looking very pleased with himself as you do it.

What a lad this very old Italian goat herder is, you think.

Tojo says nothing. Tojo looks mighty confused, you reckon. You smirk, quietly. Booze, eh? What a leveller.

As you trudge off, eventually let go by your new friend, Tojo says: 'They should bloody put that in our training, Tanky.'

'What's that, sir?'

'A good old smash-up. Our survival courses never made any mention of the therapeutic qualities of a good smash.'

You smile. 'It's an excellent point, sir.'

'I haven't felt this good in ages,' Tojo says. 'I mean, I feel rougher than a buzzard's crotch, but my spirits, Tanks, my spirits – I'm soaring.'

'Flying like a buzzard, sir,' you say.

'Well played, Tanky,' Tojo says. 'Well played.'

You walk. Seconds turn to minutes turn to hours turn to days.
You walk. Sunshine turns to clouds turns to cold turns to rain.
You walk. You walk. You walk.
One foot in front of the other –
The other foot in front of the first –
The first foot in front of the other.
Time dissolves.
Weather changes.
You sleep when you can.
And on you walk.

*

September the 23rd and Challenor is with Police Constables Peter Warwick Jay and George McIntosh Laing and they are out and about in Soho and they are looking for Joseph Oliva.

Challenor has heard that Oliva – in light of the recent arrests, not to mention Wilf Gardiner's treatment of Maria Pedrini – has threatened to firebomb the Phoenix club. Oliva, Challenor has heard, knows full well that Wilf Gardiner is doing his best to cooperate with Challenor, to grass, and help break up Oliva's little gang of racketeers and hoodlums.

That is the word on the street, so Challenor has decided to go out and make this happen, to get the arrest that he wants above all the others.

At 11 p.m. there is a sighting of Oliva in the Coffee Pot on Brewer Street with two young women, Jean Marie Murray and Jane Anna Ryan. At about 11.15, the party leaves the Coffee Pot and gets into a white Renault and drives off. Challenor, Jay and Laing are in an unmarked police car also on Brewer Street, four cars behind the white Renault.

The traffic on Brewer Street is heavy, heavier than usual, and there are some repairs being done at the Old Compton Street end, and the cars are barely moving despite the late hour. The pubs are closing, the lock-ins under way and the basement jazz clubs throbbing, and there are young men thronging in suits and shirts and ties, and women with cropped hair and cropped dresses light each other's cigarettes under streetlamps, and the queues for the basement clubs are friendly and the streets buzzing, no doubt buzzing on the cheap Yank amphetamine pills Challenor knows are being flogged by jittery young men in suits to make sure everyone has a good time.

The barely moving traffic then comes to a standstill as a lorry turns the wrong way down the one-way system on Great Windmill Street, and is consequently forced to reverse back into Brewer Street.

Challenor sees this and realises that Oliva's car is not moving and won't be for a good minute or so.

'Let's go,' Challenor says to Jay and Laing as he spears the passenger door open and runs down Brewer Street.

Challenor knocks on the passenger-side window and grins. 'Well if it ain't fucking Oliva,' he says.

Jay and Laing pull open the driver's door and Laing pulls Oliva from the driver's seat.

Challenor is showing Jean Marie Murray and Jane Anna Ryan his credentials, his warrant cards, and he's opening their doors, and he's grinning, and he's got his palms out to indicate to these lovely young women, these poor slags, he thinks, that they should remain calm and not worry and that everything is under control –

Oliva is kicking and yelling and not coming at all quietly so Laing shuts him up with his truncheon, doubles him over and buckles his knees and handcuffs him, and gets him rather more easily now over to the unmarked police car and into the back.

And Challenor brings the two women over to the unmarked police car.

Jay is searching the white Renault.

Laing hands Challenor a flick knife. 'Oliva's,' he says.

Challenor nods. 'Arrest the two girls, too,' he points at Jean Marie Murray and Jane Anna Ryan. 'Just in case he calls them as witnesses.'

Laing nods and does as Challenor says. The girls are too shocked, Challenor thinks, to make any kind of fuss.

Jay is waving from the white Renault.

He shouts, 'Guv, you need to see this!'

*

Time stretches.

Time stretches and time passes. The moments collapse into one long moment, one long reaction –

To heat, to rain, to pain, to fear –

You close your eyes from time to time and let your feet guide you, and they do, it seems, they guide you and you walk with your eyes closed and your ears and your skin, they react, and still you walk.

Weeks pass.

You are truly feral now. This Apennine range is now your home. Some days you have food; some days you do not. Some nights you sleep; some nights you do not. Some days you see the enemy, pockets of movement near villages; some days you do not.

One day, as you trudge – as the mud climbs up your trouser leg, as the rain drips down your jacket, down your collar, down your back – you realise you are no longer looking at all. Your eyes are open but you are no longer looking.

And you walk right into Tojo's back.

'Jesus,' Tojo says. 'What's the matter with you, man?'

You mumble an apology.

'Look,' Tojo is pointing ahead, 'look. What do you think?'

About a hundred yards away are a pair of German soldiers and an

Italian woman. They are huddled together in the rain and the mist, stamping their feet and lighting a cigarette, you reckon, from the shape of the huddle they have got themselves into.

'They seen us?' you ask.

Tojo's nodding. 'I reckon they have.'

They don't look too bothered, you think. Frankly, you think, you wouldn't be too bothered either, in this rain, this damp, this cold. Couple of enemies can whistle, frankly, in this bloody weather.

The two Germans flanked the woman who was clearly labouring under an enormous bundle of laundry. What a day to do the washing, you think, and you chuckle to yourself at the thought.

You can see that they have seen you.

'They've seen us, sir,' you say.

Tojo is nodding. 'We can't turn back,' he says. 'They'll definitely know we're not one of them if we do and then we'll be found in double quick time.'

You're nodding now.

Tojo says, 'We'll bluff it, hope our uniforms pass muster.'

'Right oh,' you say, and you tighten the grip on your Schmeisser, your finger curled around the trigger –

And you remember the Italian farmer poking you with his foot, and you realising that he knew straight away that your uniform was very definitely not German issue.

Could a soldier be more easily fooled?

Gawd hope so, you think.

You approach. You can see that the Germans are looking at you and are themselves looking more and more uneasy. This is clear from their manner, which is outright jumpy, and from the way they are shooting glances at each other, but neither is saying anything, and neither is saying anything to the Italian woman who is doing her very best to look down and concentrate on being weighed down by the enormous bundle of laundry.

You are metres away. The path is wide enough for you to pass –

If they – or you – yield a little.

Either side of the path there is a scattering of trees, though no real cover.

To the right, the land dips down, rolls down a slight slope. To the left, it's level for a dozen yards, then pitches up.

'Go to the right, if they engage,' Tojo says.

You nod. Your heart thumps. You're not scared. You're bloody hungry, you're bloody alive, you're itching, you're itching and you want them to bloody engage, you know that now, now that you are metres from them.

You think – if they try to stop us, I'll cut them down, but I have to fire tight, I can't hose the bullets or the Italian woman – this Italian woman who is desperately trying to pretend she isn't noticing what is happening – the Italian woman will buy it too.

Your training has prepared you, your work has prepared you, your life has prepared you. You are detached, cold. You are a bomber pilot raining death on an unseen target; there are no consequences. That is your training.

You both look like rats drowned in shit. The Germans do not like the look of you. You see their faces, their young, young faces, the same age as you, younger than you, and you can see in their young faces that they know exactly who you are.

Their faces are young and full, flabby and soft, and their figures are soft, full, flabby, they are base troops you reckon, and you can see that they have absolutely no desire, zero desire, none whatsoever to tangle with a couple of swarthy, bearded, heavily armed men.

You come abreast, they step slightly, imperceptibly back –

It's enough. You nod cheerily as you pass them, as if to reassure them there is no trouble here –

Unless they want it.

They don't.

There's a bend up ahead. You turn it, and greyhound away, sprint thirty yards, duck down behind shrubbery, wait –

Nothing. They're not coming after you.

You're not surprised. They wouldn't have stood a chance. They'd be dead before they'd unslung their rifles. Tojo was right: a skirmish, the sound of shooting, two dead bodies –

You'd be wanted men and this daytime hiking would be all over.

'They'll never report us,' Tojo says. 'They daren't. What are they going to say? That they let us stroll past without even challenging us?'

It's a fair point.

'Not a great sign though,' Tojo says, 'running into them like this.'

This is also a fair point. Makes you think, it does, this fair point, this conclusion.

Makes you bloody well think a little, about what's next, about what to do.

What are you going to do about it, though, eh?

*

Challenor quick-marches up the street back to the white Renault –

'What you got for me?' he says to Jay, who is grinning, grinning away, gurning, really, he is, like a right happy bugger.

Jay points. 'Down there, by the driver's seat, just about where Oliva's right foot would have been.'

Challenor leans through the back window. 'You smell that, son?' he asks Jay.

'I do, guv.'

'What do you think that smell might be, then, eh?'

'I'd say turpentine, guv, or gasoline, or a form of it. Turpentine my best bet.'

'I think you're right. Hang about, let's have a look at it.'

Challenor leans further in and picks up an oval-shaped bottle, which is about two thirds full with a colourless liquid. Challenor examines the bottle. It is the type of bottle, he realises, that would normally have a screw-top cap. This particular bottle, however, has no cap, no *lid*. Instead, there is a piece of towelling sticking out from the neck.

Challenor gives a manly sniff. 'It certainly does *pen*, this bottle. And this,' he gestures with the towel end of the bottle at Police Constable Peter Warwick Jay, 'is what you might call conclusive evidence of intent to wrongdoing. Wouldn't you say?'

'I would, guv.'

'Let's have him, then,' Challenor says. 'You call this in and get a squad car down and sort it here. I'll go back to the Mad House with Laing and book the fucker.'

Jay nods. 'Will do, guv.'

Challenor quick-marches back to the unmarked police car –

Oliva is handcuffed and steaming, writhing about the place, complaining, quite loudly, about the way his evening is turning out.

'You're fucked, my old beauty,' Challenor says through the window. He waves the bottle. 'You are well and truly fucked, my old son.'

'That ain't mine,' Oliva says, flatly. 'You've stitched me up.' Oliva looks at Laing. 'That weren't there when you dragged me out the car and you know it. Your guvnor's a plant.'

Laing says nothing, doesn't look at Oliva.

'You were going to use this to have a go at Gardiner's place. And these two – ' he points at the young women, the *girls* '– they'll confirm it. Both of them used to work for old Wilf. And I could mention solicitation, couldn't I, girls?'

Oliva says nothing, but he gives his two girls the old sideways fisheye, he certainly does not look too pleased that Challenor knows this about his two girls.

'Well?' Challenor says. 'You want to own up to your malicious intent now, or have I got to get you into a cell, son?'

'Cell,' Oliva says. Then: 'Fact is though, if I don't burn him, someone else will.'

Challenor grins. He slaps the roof of the car. He climbs into the passenger seat. He levers himself into the seat, folds his legs into place. 'You got enough leg room there, Oliva?'

Oliva says nothing.

'Let's jog on,' Challenor says to Laing.

Only one more to go now. Young James Fraser. Oliva's mate – Fraser the razor.

*

You're hiding out on Mamma Eliseio's farm near L'Aquila.

How you got there, you're not entirely sure.

What you do know:

Your malaria has engaged again. You think back to Algiers, when you refused to take your tablets, when you'd beaten the bloody mosquitoes through sheer will, through a triumph of the will, to coin old Adolf's phrase.

And you're jaundiced, too. You know this by the thick rust-coloured stream of urine you pissed the day before. And Tojo's feet are so bad he can hardly touch the ground with them.

You remember being led to a house in Coppito not far away. You remember injections. You remember lying on a dusty floor, shivering. You remember the doctor who tended to you, who administered these injections, you remember him performing an operation on a sow, right outside your window. You remember Tojo's feet bathed and dressed by a different doctor. Or a nurse, you're not sure. You remember practising your pidgin Italian, talking with these doctors, this nurse.

You have no idea what month it is.

What you do know:

Near L'Aquila there had been a prisoner-of-war camp, and when the Italian army surrendered, hundreds of allied POWs had scarpered and were now scattered about nearby, some of them hiding in farms like Mamma Demenica Eliseio's.

You work out you've come well over two hundred miles from where you were dropped in that cool, cool, deep-blue black night some days, weeks, months ago.

You meet three POWs who are hiding out at Mamma Eliseio's farm.

What they know:

The Allied advance has been halted at the River Sangro, and at Cassino, about eighty miles away. These POWs have heard that this state of affairs, this stalemate, may last through a cold, hard winter, through all of it. This means, you realise, looking at Tojo, that the lines are static, unmoving, and this will make it extremely hard to cross. You'd both been hoping for fluid lines.

You begin to think about leaving.

'No, no,' Mamma says. 'You stay. You stay with us.'

This seems like a very good idea indeed. You're malaria-heavy and Tojo is crippled by his blistered feet.

You hand over some money and Mamma arranges a couple of Italian suits for you. You look good. You're shivering, but you look good. And you look local.

And you settle in. You settle in for a few weeks, you keep your heads down, you help on the farm, and the war suddenly feels a long way away, and you watch as Mamma's twenty-one-year-old son Mimino becomes a man when he kills a pig with a thin blade.

And gawd knows they know how to use this slaughtered pig!

The bristles for brushes, the blood for black sausage, the nails and bones for soup, the intestines for sausage skins –

But the chops and wine for you, for all of you. More and more chops and wine –

And soon, it is Christmas. It is cold, bitterly cold, and it is Christmas.

Here you are in Italy, fifty-odd miles north-northeast of Rome, on Mamma Eliseio's farm at the southern end of the Apennine mountains, and here you are and it's bloody Christmas, and you really have no idea how that has happened.

*

'Don't hit me.'

Challenor grins. 'I ain't going to hit you, my darling. I don't think there's any need. I think this is open and shut, my old son.'

Oliva glares. 'Where are my birds?' he says. 'What have you done with them?'

'Your birds? They're with matron, your birds are. I wouldn't go calling them your birds for a bit, though. I suspect they know which side their bread is buttered, if you understand the expression, in this case.'

'Yeah, I get it, *Uncle Harry*. You're an iffy badge, a wrong 'un, a short eyes, and you'll see to it they'll sign whatever it is you want them to. That about right, is it?'

Challenor nods. 'I'd say so, yes, love. That. Is. About. Right.'

Oliva nods. 'Well, you know what I'll say.'

'Do I?'

'Course you do, detective. You've framed me with that bottle and you and your cronies know it. Do me a favour, Uncle Harry,' he says, 'it's clear as a bell you've got the needle to us.'

Challenor sniffs and clears his throat. 'What's that cologne? Eau de Ponce?'

Oliva ignores Challenor, goes on. 'You get my brief and we can get this sorted.' Now, he smiles. Challenor sees him smile. And this sparks something in Challenor. He waits. Oliva says, 'It ain't a problem, Harry. I won't bring anything against you, a complaint, charges or whatnot. We'll just pretend this never happened.' He takes a step closer to Challenor. 'No reason we can't work together, in my mind. *Sai cosa intendo?*'

'Yeah, I know what you mean. *Ma che sei grullo*, young man.'

Oliva raises his eyebrows at that one, Challenor notices. He learned that from a lad in Italy: you must be joking, was the basic translation. Having a laugh.

'You don't like us wops, do you, Harry?'

Challenor glares, now. He is not having that. He is not having any of that. He is not going to mess about anymore, Challenor. 'Maria Pedrini's a nice bird,' he says. '*She* one of yours?'

'Now why you got to mention Maria, eh?'

'Answer the question.'

'Well, it depends, dunnit. Depends on the day, on the circumstances, you know, on the situation.'

'She'll turn, you know,' Challenor says. 'She's about two thirds there already, I reckon.' He pauses. 'Least she was when I last saw her.' He makes a salacious face, a vulgar face, a very unambiguous kind of face. 'Very private, that little church of yours, innit? Comfortable little crypt, eh?'

Oliva has balled his fists. 'You shut your mouth.'

'Yeah, she's fiery, young Maria. It wasn't easy.' Challenor points at his neck: there is a reddening scratch and soft-looking bruise. Self-inflicted, not ten minutes before he paid Oliva this visit, but who's to know. 'See that? Smarts, it does.'

'You fucking – '

'She'll turn on the lot of you now. Riccardo too. All I got to do is put the word out she's tainted goods. *Sai cosa intendo?*'

Oliva grunts and turns and picks up the chair in the cell. 'You're not going to hit me, Uncle fucking Harry,' he yells, 'as I've eaten bigger blokes than you!'

He comes at Challenor, the chair above his head. Challenor moves, deftly, to the side, pivots on his right foot, swings his

---

shoulders round to avoid Oliva's charge, and brings his hand down hard in a chop on Oliva's neck, his *windpipe*.

Oliva is knocked back, drops the chair.

Challenor takes one step, and plants his boot in Oliva's stomach. Oliva gasps and rolls into the foetal position, clutching himself.

Challenor takes off his jacket. Challenor leans over him.

Challenor spits in his ear. 'I'm going to enjoy this, sunshine. *Bel ragazzo.*'

Later, Challenor thinks about Mamma Eliseio, how he owes her his life, when it comes down to it. And bloody hell if she and hers weren't brave! They'd have done anything for Tanky and Tojo, and anyone else sticking it to the Krauts, Challenor reckons. And lucky too. Snouts everywhere, there were, bleating sheep, any number of possible grasses – you got in with the Krauts and they made it worth your while.

They certainly didn't mess about when it came to reprisals.

Challenor remembers what happened on March 23rd, 1944.

The Italian partisans in Rome went and lobbed a homemade bomb at an SS unit, and thirty-three of the Germans bought it. The Krauts did not like that one bit. The next day, they rounded up three hundred and thirty-five Italian civilians and took them down to a spot in the Ardeatine caves. It was quiet down there, Challenor heard, a murky spot for a murky business. The Krauts only went and executed the lot, massacred the poor sods, shot dead as a simple act of revenge. Thirty-three SS; we'll have ten times your lot, was the thinking. Crummy bastards.

Thank God for Mamma Eliseio and her family.

Thank God for the good fortune and the good Italians that kept Challenor alive.

*

Christmas Eve itself is a grand old smash-up, crikey, they know how to hold a village celebration, they do –

Not the war, not the freezing weather, nothing is going to get in the way of the traditional festivities, as neighbour calls upon neighbour, thrusting their wine like weapons, and drinking their way through the village.

And you're getting drunker and drunker, you are, reeling from the whole affair, you are, really tucking in, really biting *into this good wine. And you're feeling bold in your Italian suit, and you don't half look good, that's for sure, in this new Italian suit, this slicked-back dark hair you're sporting, and the nice smell you've got on, that nice drop of cologne. And young Anita, Mamma's nineteen-year-old daughter, is almost certainly giving you the eye, and you reckon she might want seeing to, but you can't, you really can't bring yourself to give her one, not now, you can't step up now, not after everything the family's done for you, it wouldn't be right, wouldn't be polite, to give her one, not now, even if she is, quite clearly, quite clearly giving you the eye.*

You decide that the best course of action here is to resolutely pour your attention all over the red wine and to drink yourself into such an almighty stupor that any eye-giving is rendered futile. Get so drunk, in fact, that if she does continue to give you the eye, in your eyes, you'll be seeing about a half dozen of hers.

Tojo is also applying himself and is trying out his own Italian on anyone who'll listen, and the party winds its way through the village and then you're propelled towards a large wooden door, and you're pouring yourself into the village church for Midnight Mass.

OK, then, why not? You can't make out a word of the little service book you're given, but why not?

'When in Rome, eh, sir?' you say to Tojo and this is so funny, so gloriously funny, so epically amusing, so classically brilliant in its wit, so English *in its classical wit, that you laugh very, very loudly indeed.*

Heads turn. Your village friends take up the laughter, very, very loudly, and you are deeply confused. Why do they think it's so funny?

The laughter continues, there are cheers, wine is poured down necks –

Then it settles and a couple of your village chums nod, reassuringly.

The singing starts. You look across the aisle and your blood freezes –

Rows of field-grey uniforms. Rows of field-grey uniforms who are now ignoring you. Rows of field-grey uniforms stiffly chorusing the Christmas hymns.

You sit tight. You wear your civvy suit and you sit tight.

You wish for sobriety –

And a simple army-issue knife.

And after the service the rows of field-grey uniforms are pelting each other with snowballs. Villagers join in. You grope in the snow for a rock, a rock you can wrap in snow. You bend down, and you fall over and there is laughter.

Lying in the snow you yell, 'God didn't hear you, you bastards!'

Then Tojo is pulling you up and pulling you away and you're poured onto the hay in your barn and then –

*

Midnight, September 25th, and Police Constable Donald Francis Gibson and Police Constable Michael Margrave Trowbridge Edwards have got James Fraser in the charge room.

And Challenor is on his way down.

Fraser the Razor, he's thinking, the last one, the final link. Then we can put this ugly, sordid little mess to bed.

Initial report states that Police Constables Gibson and Edwards were keeping observation at the Phoenix club when Fraser approached. As he approached, Wilf Gardiner pointed him out to the policemen. Fraser, the report states, was holding something in his pocket and, as *he* approached Gardiner, he said, 'I've been looking for you, you bastard.'

Constable Gibson promptly stopped and searched Fraser, finding on his person, in his pocket, a cut-throat razor. Of course he did, Challenor thinks. Fraser is then reported to have said, 'I suppose he put you on to me, then?' Meaning Gardiner. 'He doesn't know what's coming to him. He'll have to get more than you lot to look after him. His days are numbered.'

Challenor decides to make this snappy. He bullies his way into the charge room and dismisses Police Constable Donald Francis Gibson and Police Constable Michael Margrave Trowbridge Edwards.

'Let's make this snappy, my old darling.' He points at the razor. 'This is yours.'

Fraser nods. 'It is mine, yes. It's for cutting banana stalks and twine. Know where I work?'

'No, I do not.'

'Covent Garden, guv. I need this razor for my job, like I says, cutting banana stalks and twine.'

'Fair enough,' Challenor says. 'Well, either way, it's going to look good when placed alongside your previous, that little pistol you had with no firearms certificate.'

Fraser reflects on this.

'And let's not forget your little nickname, my old son. No smoke and all that, you know what I mean?'

'What exactly do you want?' Fraser says.

'Have a seat, son,' Challenor says. Fraser sits down. Challenor takes a couple of paces around the room, then leans in very close, very close to Fraser's face, Fraser's very close-shaven face. 'I want you and your pals on racketeering, on protection charges, on demanding money with menaces and on possession of a fair few offensive weapons. That, my love, will do me. *That* is what I want and that is what I'm going to get.'

'Fair enough,' says Fraser. He nods. 'I guess it's game on, then? You'll have to get up very early to catch us out, Uncle Harry.'

Challenor smiles. Challenor quite likes the cut – excuse the pun – of Fraser the Razor's jib, quite likes his style. 'I guess it is. You know where you are, you'll get your brief – and I'll get the lot of you. I know exactly where you're putting the bite on.' Challenor whistles and Constable Gibson pokes his head round the door. 'Take this one to his lodgings will you, Gibson, please?'

'Certainly, sir.'

Challenor looks at Fraser. 'You've got a decision to make, son. You let me know when you've made it, OK?'

Fraser nods. Fraser leaves quietly.

Challenor grins.

*

Next day, Christmas Day, and your head is –

You know the drill. Your head is drilling. Your head is absolutely drilling. It's absolutely, positively drilling –

It's drilling into your head, your head is.

Your brain and mind –

They're being drilled by your head, they are.

And yet you can hear a lot of movement, a lot of shouting and some gunfire and you know those field-grey uniforms are out and about and you know what that means.

You and Tojo have a war council. It all feels a bit close, suddenly, after the night before, it all feels a bit bloody close, *a bit edgy, really, there is a lot of edge about, you think, some serious* edge, *and it's not just the shaking violence of your hangover.*

You need to take the edge off, somehow.

Tojo knows:

You need to move and you need to split up. Tojo will go with a woman called Filomena to a hideout at her gaff. You will go to one of the little rat-infested grottos in the outer ring of the farm.

Job done. Cheers, Tojo, good luck and see you on the other side.

The lines – see you on the other side of the lines.

Tojo smiles, grimly. 'Good luck, Tanky,' he says. 'Well done.'

And that's that.

Your grotto is lined with hay. You settle in and practise your burgeoning Italian and busy yourself with not being nibbled at by the rats.

Anita brings you food, once a day. It is a glorious twenty minutes when she sits with you and you wolf pasta and wine and she prattles on in Italian, Italian which you are beginning to understand, you reckon. And when you've stuffed your gob with her pasta, you engage in a little conversation and you're definitely getting a little better at this lark.

The routine lasts three days.

December 28th: Anita brings news –

Tojo has been discovered and taken. Filomena, the poor cow, has been executed for hiding him. Silly, silly slag, she is: what did she go and do that for, offering to hide him, getting herself executed. You nod, grimly. You force back a tear. You cannot afford to think about this beyond what it is: a practicality.

You tell Anita that now you must go –

She nods. She knows. She has a message from Mamma. She relates it: Go with Anita until the Popoli road. Then go –

Godspeed.

Fair enough. It changes quickly, war. It changes that quickly. You're alone, now. You're all alone.

*

December 1962.

Challenor sits in his office. Radio's playing 'Big Girls Don't Cry' by Frankie Valli and his mob. They're back at number one,

Challenor notes. He listens to old Frankie crooning away about how it's got nothing to do with you, and how he hopes the old girl knows this.

Except right now it feels like *everything* has to do with Challenor.

The Old Bailey, the *fucking* Old Bailey, no less, is currently hosting, is currently in the middle of, the trial of a certain Soho gang, a gang that is comprised primarily of Oliva and Pedrini and Ford and Cheeseman and Fraser.

Challenor's on edge, he's a touch edgy, he is. And he is controlling this edge with regular doses of Guinness, and regular pills, regular pills as prescribed by the police doctor to help him with his anxiety and stress, anxiety and stress initially caused by traumatic experiences behind enemy lines during the Second World War. Battle Fatigue, or, sometimes, Combat Stress Reaction, is what they call it now, he thinks.

And it's this condition of his that is keeping him from the trial. Challenor will not give evidence in person. His statements have been made, documented, signed and corroborated.

And it's in the Crown's best interest that Challenor steers clear.

Challenor does not like this. He does not.

When things get hot, get going, Challenor likes to do, to act. He is twitching, now, Challenor, waiting to see what happens.

He does not like it one bit, when things are out of his control.

*

You're alone and walking towards Chieti, towards the Adriatic, and bombs are shrieking down all around you. RAF raid, which at once warms and alarms you –

After all this, you think, I do not want, I absolutely do not want, after all this, to be flattened by one of my own bombs! What an absolute slag, you think, to be killed by one of your own. You refuse, you wholeheartedly refuse to be squashed by one of your own, made-in-Blighty bombs that are screaming from the sky and falling all around you, pulling and tearing the ground all about the place and making buildings shudder, making them tremble then collapse, like the knock-out punch you land on your opponent and you watch as his knees wobble, his knees go, and he topples, slowly, wobbly-kneed, over and out. The knees of a lot of buildings are going right now, you think. There's a lot of wobbling and toppling going on. They haven't got the legs, these buildings.

And you're shaking and shivering with the malaria, and it's raining, and there are German staff cars tearing down the roads, and you're spending more and more time in ditches and under bushes, wet, cold rain dripping down your back.

You crawl into an abandoned house, half of it simply not there, taken by one of these bombs you're avoiding. You're very busy avoiding these bombs. You find a fireplace. You find an old chair. You break the chair into pieces. You tear up bits of the skirting board. You light a fire. You lie next to it. You shiver. You sweat –

You sleep.

You sleep like a milk-drunk pup. You can actually feel yourself falling asleep – you fall *asleep, fall into a deep, deep sleep –*

And then you wake – sharp.

You wake with a stinging, hot pain in your back, a sharp, stinging, hot pain, a pain like the stab of red-hot needles.

You wake to the smell of burning cloth.

It takes a moment to put the two sensations – the pain, the awful pain; the smell, the awful smell – together, to understand that your coat is on fire.

Your coat, you understand, is on fire.

You tear it off, tear at it, shake it off you and beat down the flames. There is a large hole in the back.

There is no more wood.

It is almost midnight.

You review your situation. It does not look good, you decide. Some might say, you think, that it looks decidedly hopeless, your situation.

If you stay, you will die, of frostbite or of malaria.

You have a coat with a hole in it. You have no food. You have no water. You're alone in a village crawling with Germans, a whole gang of field-grey uniforms crawling all about the place.

It's not much of a dilemma.

You're going to try and make it – now, right now – to Chieti.

*

December 18th, 1962.

Oliva and Pedrini and Ford and Cheeseman and Fraser:

Guilty.

For conspiracy to demand money with menaces, demanding money with menaces, and possessing offensive weapons:

Pedrini is sentenced to seven years' imprisonment. Cheeseman is sentenced to three years' imprisonment.

For conspiracy to demand money with menaces, and for demanding money with menaces:

Ford is sentenced to five years' imprisonment.

For conspiracy to demand money with menaces, for possessing an offensive weapon, and for receiving a stolen radio:

Oliva is sentenced to six years' imprisonment.

For possessing an offensive weapon:

Fraser is sentenced to fifteen months' imprisonment.

In his office, Challenor punches the air. Challenor grins.

Challenor reads Judge Maude's statement on passing sentence.

It is necessary for the protection of the public that blackmail of any kind – particularly in the heart of London – should be sternly dealt with at the earliest possible stage – that is, when persons have only gone as far as agreeing to commit such a detestable crime. In other words, when they conspire to commit blackmail.

Moreover, the punishment must be of such severity as will show that the courts are of determination to strike fear into the hearts of persons who agree to act as 'frighteners' and thieves. Doubtless you thought that with Mr Gardiner's disgraceful past, he would not dare to invoke the law and face the police and jury for the fear in his heart that the past would prevent the acceptance of the truth from his lips.

Woe betide anyone if anything happens to Mr Gardiner and woe betide anyone who tries to do this sort of thing again in the heart of London. The next time, the sentences will be doubled.

Challenor likes the touch of mentioning Gardiner like this. It's a nice touch, that. Good old his honourable Judge Maude.

Challenor is also very pleased with the headline in the *Evening Standard*:

'Sergeant Harry topples "King Oliva".'

Yeah, cheers, Challenor thinks, raising a can of celebratory Guinness to the photo of himself in the paper, in which he is raising a glass of celebratory Guinness.

Yeah, have that, you flash Italian fucks.

*

You can't take more than about five steps at a time before another German vehicle rumbles along the road towards you and you have to dive into the ice-covered ditch.

You stumble and trip and fall and drag yourself along this road, this endless road bustling with German vehicles –

And then you walk straight into a torch, straight into a sentry's torch.

You're at the edge of a village, a perimeter patrolled by German sentries, a village that you didn't even notice as you stumbled, exhausted, towards it, cold, exhausted, shaking and shivering from your malaria and you are falling apart, it feels, your malaria and you don't have the legs, your malarial knees have gone, the malaria, this is, that you can't overcome by willpower alone.

The German sentry is poking his gun at you, he's shouting, barking at you. You're shaking your head. He pulls an Italian over from the hut behind him. The Italian speaks at you, fast, this Italian speaks at a hell of a pace, Christ, you can't follow much and the game is almost certainly up.

You're exhausted. You shrug. 'Englander, Englander,' you hear yourself saying.

Then: hands all over you, the gun, the silk map.

You hear: 'You are armed, equipped with a map and wearing civilian clothes. This is a serious matter.'

Then: the back of a car and the SS headquarters in Popoli.

'You are not a soldier,' an officer is saying to you as he leads you across a courtyard stained with blood, a courtyard whose walls are pockmarked with bullet holes. 'You are a spy and you will be shot if you do not help us. We want to know what you have been doing and where you have been.'

Then the beatings start.

*

Challenor swaggers down the corridors of the Mad House. He saunters, he *struts*. He's peacocking about the place, lording it. This stroll around the Mad House is a bloody victory parade.

Challenor is brandishing a copy of the *Evening News*, brandishing it like a truncheon, like a conductor's baton, thrusting it under his arm like Nelson's telescope.

It's a bloody victory parade, it is. It's an open-top bus of a stroll.

Challenor's reciting the newspaper report as he parades around West End Central, accepting the handshakes and the accolades, the backslaps and the grins, the earnest nods and the winks.

The newspaper's report is favourable, Challenor reckons. Favourable is definitely a good word for this report. It is approving, *auspicious*. Challenor loves this report, bloody loves it, though of course he wasn't *actually* there, wasn't actually listening.

Listening to the sentences being passed was forty-one-year-old Det.-Sgt Harry Challenor, who had been assigned to break the protection gangs in the West End.

Sgt Challenor, holder of the Military Medal, heavyweight boxer and swimmer and an ex-Paratrooper, led a team of detectives. He was helped by his knowledge of Italian learned during the war, in interviewing Soho's cosmopolitan population.

*

You're in Italy, in a cell with a dirty mattress, in the SS headquarters at Popoli, not thirty miles from Allied lines. You're naked and curled into the foetal position, you're naked with split and swollen lips, your body one vast ache –

And two SS goons are beating the living daylights out of you.

You are being handed a right old leathering.

Part Two

TRIUMPH OF THE WILL

January 1963 – July 1964

Loon

'You like animals?' Tanky asks me, the second time I meet him.

'Well,' I say.

'You should, like animals, I mean. They're all right, animals.'

'OK.' I'm not sure what to say next. You're often not sure what to say next to Tanky.

'You got any pets? Pets are staunch.'

'Yeah, I have.'

'What is it?'

'Cat.'

'Umm,' says Tanky. He pulls a face that seems to say: not sure about that, son. 'Bit moody, cats,' he says. 'I've got a pet. You wanna know what it is?'

I nod.

'It's a parrot.'

I laugh. I'm only eleven and the idea of a pet parrot is a hoot.

'What's funny?' Tanky asks.

'A pet parrot – I don't know,' I say.

'He's a good lad, my parrot. He's called Darren.'

I laugh again. Even louder this time. 'Darren the parrot! Darren the parrot!' I yell.

Tanky smiles. 'Guess what I feed him?' he asks. 'He's got a top diet Darren has.'

'Er,' I say. 'Parrots eat – carrots!'

Tanky laughs. 'Good one. Try again.'

'Parrots eat – '

My grandad walks in. 'Polyfilla,' he says.

Tanky roars.

'I don't get it,' I say.

'Not to worry,' Tanky says. 'Anyway, you'll never guess it. Darren eats fried eggs. And drinks Guinness.'

I look at my grandad. He smiles, nods.

'Fried eggs and Guinness,' I say. 'Crikey.'

'Just like me,' says Tanky. 'Fried eggs and Guinness.'

Five

'As a CID officer, I thought he was great. I had the greatest respect
for him. He was nicking the right people at the right time.'
Maurice Harding, Detective Constable, West End Central

Challenor sits in his office, high up in his throne.

The king is dead. Long live the king. King Challenor.

Challenor thinks of the old line:

Oh, what a tangled web we weave
When first we practice to deceive

Challenor knows there are rumours. There are the minor ones, that this Soho protection gang that Challenor has put away is just a bunch of kid no-hopers, a few chancers and wide boys, not really dealing with anything of any substance, any weight. After all, these rumours are saying, they were into old Wilf for a hundred nicker, loose change, fuck all. So, there's that one.

The other one is a little punchier. Wilf's doorman, a Mr Berrill, has been mouthing off, apparently. He's been talking, been running his mouth – he knew all along, he's saying, *days* in advance, that a knife, a razor and a bottle of turps would be uncovered. What he's been putting about with his quick mouth is that Old Wilf paid a lot of money to make sure these goods were found on the young gentlemen of the Soho protection gang.

Challenor doesn't like this rumour.

Fortunately, the rumour is proving no more popular among Challenor's seniors, or Challenor's colleagues.

Challenor is Harry the Brave, right now. He's top dog, Challenor.

He's also still The Stranger at home. This troubles him. Doris has been supportive of his success, he can't deny that, give her credit, but she seems to now expect that he'll be calming down a bit, letting some others take the lead, put in the hours, put in a shift.

It's like she doesn't know him at all.

He knows that's not true and he knows she doesn't really expect him to lessen his work – she just *hopes* he will. Hope over expectation.

And it's not like Challenor's chasing skirt or anything like that. He's not done that for a long time, not really since his Watford days. And he's never been one to really *chase* skirt, as in extra-marital skirt, he thinks. He's wandered along *next* to one or two, been led down a path once or twice, but he's never really *chased*. He's always thought it seemed like too much hassle, too much *admin*, having another bird on the go. That's what he says, to the lads, at least, when it becomes clear that he is not one for the ladies, that he is not a *ladies'* man.

Truth is, he's been in love only once, with Doris, and, at forty-odd years old, he's realised the fundamental truth of that, and with fundamental truth comes a fundamental position: no extra-curriculars, no disrespect, no raising of any hands.

That last one has been true his whole life, Challenor thinks. After watching his old man, Tom Challenor the steelworks Staffordshire bull terrier, laying into his mum or his sister, verbals, in the main, but terrifying, or disciplining young Harry with leather belt and clenched fist, applying low blows, to stomach, to groin, where the pain is worst of all, and where no teacher or neighbour will ever see any injuries.

He got his beer though, and things weren't too bad, Challenor reflects. Never any dough, of course, and they'd skipped from house to house to avoid creditors, to start 'afresh' and whatnot.

Doris doesn't know too much of this, Challenor thinks. He's not one to share too much. Watford childhood, sports – football, athletics and boxing – lather boy in the local barber shop.

She does know about Challenor's occasionally erratic behaviour though. That's for sure. She's seen enough of his, what they call, delusional moments, when he's not quite sure if things are happening, or are a part of a memory. Not many people know about this – and Challenor likes to keep it that way. Not too many know what he went through in the war, not in Italy, at least. France, sure, that's world famous what he did there, Operation Wallace, but Italy remains dark, *cloaked*.

There are rumours, he knows that, but they're tame enough, they're not too wild, these rumours, just your basic ex-SAS hardman type of thing, your basic psycho, but *our* psycho, a psycho on the right team. Challenor doesn't mind these rumours too much.

Fact is though, he's got a new project so Doris is going to have to extend her saintly patience a touch further.

Challenor's examining a file on a certain Lionel 'Curly' King, an ex-con, wrongly imprisoned – served a two stretch before the pardon – and desperate and now working at a bookies.

And one of his employer's shops was recently blown up. And another – even more recently – was found to have an unexploded bomb in a back room.

Challenor fancies he can turn this Lionel 'Curly' King.

He needs a new grass, a new snitch – and he's recruiting. And Lionel 'Curly' King's got all the credentials, including past business relationships with Wilf Gardiner and Johnnie Ford.

Challenor fancies this Lionel 'Curly' King and reckons he might be the way in to the next level of Soho gang.

Really clean up the bastards.

That's the goal, anyway, the aim.

The Scourge of Soho – he likes the sound of that.

*

There is a boot in your side. Thump.

There is a boot in your back. Crack.

There is a boot in your middle. Gasp.

There are fists to your face, to your stomach, to your balls –

You're naked and bleeding. You're curled up and your face is set in grim determination. This cunt is not going to hurt you.

You hear: get up, Harry, you little shit. Son of mine?

Thump.

Call yourself a Challenor?

Crack.

You fucking what? You fucking talk, will you?

You raise your head –

Smack.

You see: two black uniforms –

On the shoulder of one the death head insignia of an officer –

On the collar of the other, twin lightning flashes.

You hear: you are not a soldier, you are a spy and you will be shot if you don't help us.

You vow: I will never be a prisoner.

*

Lionel 'Curly' King has called West End Central as he's heard that the police want to question him about the explosion in the betting shop on Greek Street, where he is currently employed, and about the detonators and other suspicious equipment found in the betting shop on Percy Street, where he is also employed, employed in both instances by old 'Major' Collins, a right naughty man, he used to be, this 'Major' Collins, Challenor has heard.

Lionel 'Curly' King has been told that he is not under any sort of suspicion, not a *suspect*, as such, and that he is only wanted for questioning to, you know, what's the phrase, *to assist the police with their enquiries* –

That's the official line, at least.

Thing is, what Mr King doesn't yet know is that when he reports at West End Central to help the police with their enquiries, he will be directed – directly – to Detective Sergeant Harold Challenor's office to have, as they say, *unofficially*, a quiet word.

Challenor's sitting in his office, waiting, sitting with a tasty grin plastered across his mug, sipping a creamy, frankly filthy coffee, a coffee definitely *not* from his favoured Italian grinders, content in the knowledge that Mr King is at present only a few corridors away and will be with him very shortly indeed.

Radio's on –

That intergalactic bleep of a melody by Joe Meek's mob, what's it called? Challenor puzzles. Challenor scratches the old bonce. Telstar, that's it, he thinks, bloody thing's been number one for weeks. Sounds like a vacuum cleaner on the blink, Challenor reckons. Hardly the rhythm and blues future predicted by old Wilf Gardiner. Challenor can't imagine anyone pissing themselves to this. It's like listening to a fairground ride.

'Sir?'

Challenor looks up. Police Constable Peter Warwick Jay has popped his head around the door, as Challenor requested he did so, not five minutes ago.

'Peter,' Challenor says, 'do come in.' Challenor grins. He nods at the ceiling. 'You like this tune, Peter, this *ditty*?'

Police Constable Peter Warwick Jay appears confused. 'Sir?' he says.

'There's no right answer, Peter,' Challenor says. Challenor hasn't told Jay why he is here in Challenor's office, so Challenor understands the young man's confusion, especially considering

Challenor's history of somewhat – what's the word? – somewhat *erratic* behaviour. Challenor's reputation doesn't half precede him, he knows that.

'Well, I – I suppose I do, yes, sir,' young Jay says.

'You're not alone, Peter,' Challenor says. 'It's doing rather well, I believe, in the old, you know, what's the badger, the old hit parade.'

'It is, sir, yes. I believe it is.'

'Bloody racket if you ask me,' Challenor says. 'Where's the swing, where's the *soul*, eh? Know what I mean?'

'I suppose I do, sir.'

Challenor smiles. 'Sit down, Peter, over there, if you'd be so.' He points to a chair in the corner of his office. 'You're going to do me a little favour, old son.'

'Anything, sir.'

'Good lad. Now sit down. And take this.' Challenor hands Police Constable Peter Warwick Jay a notepad and paper. 'Peter,' Challenor says, 'you sit tight, act as a witness, and take plentiful notes while I interview a young hoodlum called Lionel King, "Curly" to his associates, on account, I believe, of his hairstyle. OK?'

Police Constable Peter Warwick Jay nods.

'They say he's had a perm, this lad King, that's what they say. A *perm*. What's it coming to, eh, Peter?'

'Not sure, sir, to be honest.'

'Quite.'

Challenor busies himself. He jerks his chin at the notepad and paper on Police Constable Peter Warwick Jay's lap. 'You know the drill.'

Jay nods.

He's all right, Police Constable Peter Warwick Jay is, Challenor thinks, quite all right.

He knows the drill.

*

You groan. You wake. You moan. You shake.

You ache.

You hear voices. You hear questions. You hear your father. You hear words forming questions. You hear voices forming words forming questions. Get up, you hear your father saying, get up, you miserable little fuck, get up –

You say nothing. You eat nothing. You drink nothing.

Time passes. You think this thought –

Time passes. It has never felt so true.

The beatings are repeated.

The questions are repeated.

You ache.

You ache –

You grin.

*

Challenor's looking at Lionel 'Curly' King.

Police Constable Peter Warwick Jay is looking at his notepad and pen.

Lionel 'Curly' King is looking at Challenor.

Challenor's not sure he quite appreciates the cut of Lionel 'Curly' King's jib. There's the perm, for a start: a great shrub of hair, a sandy wheatsheaf, a cascade of ringlets, a real *bush*.

'Know why you're here, do you, Lionel?' Challenor says.

King smiles. 'I know why I'm here in West End Central, yes.' He pauses. 'I don't know why I'm in your office though, Detective Challenor. I didn't know this business was a part of your racket.'

Challenor smiles. No, he thinks, he does not like the cut of Lionel 'Curly' King's jib at all. Quite the opposite, in reality, he acknowledges to himself. Fact is, he is quite unimpressed with the cut of Lionel 'Curly' King's jib. This young man, he thinks, is a little pleased with himself, a little *full* of himself. Challenor glances at Jay and sees he is scribbling one or two notes and he guesses that these notes are likely along the same lines as Challenor's thoughts.

'Soho's salubrious and upstanding criminal enterprises of any sort are of interest to me, young man,' Challenor says. 'Quite apart from the fact that you're a known associate of my former friends and sparring partners Joseph Oliva and Johnnie Ford, and some kind of former colleague or, perhaps, *employee* of that dirty bastard Wilf Gardiner. Quite apart from these two pieces of information, you get out the nick, get a job, and within months, your employer suffers a couple of not insignificant incidents, one of which involves his poor, hardworking bookmakers blowing up. So you can see why I'd want to see you.'

King nods. King sits up straight, eyes dead ahead. King lights a cigarette. King says, 'I thought you fancied me as a grass. *Uncle Harry.*'

Challenor matches King's stare. 'You're a silly, silly boy, my old son, saying something like that, implying something like that, what with a brother officer here taking down all the particulars, acting as a witness.'

'Not true then?' King asks.

Challenor grins. 'Why don't we start with why you felt you had the right to intervene on July 17th of last year in an altercation between Johnnie Ford and Wilf Gardiner. You got them to shake hands. Why?'

King says nothing. King shrugs.

'You don't feel the need to answer this?'

King shakes his hand. 'Obvious, innit.'

Challenor says, 'Don't monkey about, matey. I'm not sure that it is. Strikes me that you were using your influence to help along the deal Ford and Oliva were doing with Gardiner, a scam, a spot of intimidation, a little protection money. Strikes me, in fact, that we can stick that mediation on you, fit you right up, in fact, considering the sentences your little friends received. Shouldn't be too hard, my old darling, to mediate *that* kind of a deal, at our end at least.'

King looks unfazed. Challenor's not too keen on this. King says, 'You heard this little fiction, did you?'

Challenor leans forward. Challenor narrows his eyes. 'Witnessed. I know you were blagging, and I know where else you were trying it on. It's in a report. Likely you and your mob didn't know we had old Wilf's places under surveillance. I suspect,' and Challenor looks at Jay, 'I suspect – and correct me if I'm wrong, Peter – that we could have that report sent up in not longer than twenty or so minutes. That right, Peter?'

'I'd say so, guv,' says Police Constable Peter Warwick Jay.

Challenor nods, quite vigorously. 'So you see, young man, you're in something of a pickle.'

King says nothing. Police Constable Peter Warwick Jay says nothing. Challenor says nothing.

The atmosphere in the room, Challenor thinks, is *thick*. There's a soupy quality to this new atmosphere, in fact, a real fog in here, Challenor notes, a dense cloud of atmosphere.

Challenor says, 'I want information, my old son, information that comes from *inside* the betting shop as to why they were bombed. And you're going to get me that information.'

King says nothing.

'Am I not making myself clear, Lionel?' Challenor says.

King nods. 'Crystal, Uncle Harry. Thing is though, I only work there, and I don't have nothing to do with anything else. You know what? You're best off talking to my employer, he'd know more than me.' King pauses. He lights another cigarette. 'Though hang about, haven't you already spoken to him?'

Challenor does not like this answer at all, not one bit.

Challenor stands and leans over his desk. He brings his fist down onto his desk very hard indeed. He bangs his desk with his fist five times, each time harder than the time before.

Challenor snorts. Challenor blazes. Challenor *throbs*. 'That is not a satisfactory answer, Lionel,' he says. 'Not satisfactory at all.'

Challenor straightens. Challenor moves out from behind his desk and stands behind Lionel 'Curly' King. Challenor *seethes*.

Police Constable Peter Warwick Jay sits tight. Challenor sees the calm in Police Constable Peter Warwick Jay and is reassured.

'This your natural colour, is it, son?' Challenor asks King, his hand flicking at King's hair, his hair*style*.

'Don't see many lads with a barnet like yours, Lionel. What's done it for you, eh? You trying to look like a bird? Or a *darkie*, eh? That what it's about, a lack of character or something? You weren't breastfed? That it?'

King says nothing.

Challenor continues. Challenor *snarls*. 'I do not mess about, young man. I certainly do not mess about. You, my old darling, may think you can play me for a fool, but you certainly cannot, as I do not, I repeat, do not, mess about.'

Challenor's massaging King's shoulders now. 'You enjoying this, Lionel? You like my hands on you, do you? Well, son, you will feel my hands on you, soon enough, if you don't do what you're bloody well told.'

King's tensed up, Challenor can feel, with his hands on him. And not surprising, Challenor thinks. He's raging, after all, Challenor. He *burns*.

'Now this case is my case, Mr King, regardless of what you might or might not have been told, this is my fucking case and no one, not you, not any of my colleagues, and certainly not any of your two-bob Soho gangster mates, is going to tell me any different. You got that?'

King nods. About bloody time, Challenor thinks.

'So you are going to get the information to which I earlier alluded, and you're going to tell me, and only me, when you've found out what I need to know. You'll just be another snout in Soho. I run more here than there are on Old MacDonald's farm, isn't that right, Peter?'

Police Constable Peter Warwick Jay nods. 'That's right, guv.'

Challenor goes on. 'And if you don't do that, Lionel – and sharpish, mind, I want this *pronto*, right? – you will find yourself in more than just a pickle, my friend. You will find yourself in an awful lot of trouble indeed.' Challenor pauses. He moves from behind King and sits back down at his desk. 'We in agreement, Lionel?' he asks.

King nods.

'Say it, Lionel, if you will?'

'We are in agreement, Detective Challenor.'

Challenor smiles. 'Off you go, son,' he says. 'Do one.'

Lionel 'Curly' King does one. He's out of there in a shot.

Challenor looks at Police Constable Peter Warwick Jay.

'Thank you, Peter, you were outstanding. Type up your notes for me, please, if you, you know, if you *will*.' Challenor winks. 'Let's get this agreement down on the page, eh?' he says. 'At least regarding young Lionel's haircut.'

Police Constable Peter Warwick Jay nods and grins.

Challenor roars with laughter at his own joke.

*

You're grinning as your boys in the RAF are paying Popoli another visit –

Bombs rain down. Bombs whine and fall and crash and wallop into the town, into the roads, into the courtyards, into the buildings around you, into, it feels, the building that you're in –

Into the tanks, into the trucks, into the staff cars –

Into the soldiers, into the officers, into the domestic staff –

But you're quite safe in your little cell, it appears.

You jump up to the window, jump up to the barred window, grab the bars in the window, and stick your mug in between them, stick your grinning mug in between the bars –

And you don't half laugh, laugh at the chaos, laugh at the chaos and the carnage, laugh at the panic, laugh at the damage, the panic and the ugly, ugly damage.

'Go on, my son!' you shout, as you hear another plane overhead, another bomb on its way down.

'Go on, get stuck in, don't be shy, get stuck in, son!' you shout, gleeful and roaring you are, roaring with laughter.

You're howling at the moon –

You're howling at the moon, urging your boys on, half-mad and happy –

Then: the skitter of bullets on concrete, on brick –

And close by. Too bloody close!

You look down. A Jerry officer has spotted you, a sergeant you think, on reflection, has spotted you howling and laughing and roaring and he's having none of it. His Luger's out and he's aiming right at your window, your barred window, right where your gurning face is sticking out –

You jump back down. You're still laughing –

'Christ,' you're thinking, 'they'll have your bloody guts for garters for that!'

Laughing as bits of their gaff are blown to smithereens, some of their mob blown to smithereens, some of their friends killed in fairly spectacular and highly unpleasant fashion by the bombs of your boys in the RAF, and there you are laughing it up –

This will not go down at all well, you think.
But you're OK. They've missed you, your boys.
Good lads, your boys. Staunch.

*

It's been a couple of days since the meeting with Lionel 'Curly' King, the walking hairstyle, the *perm*, and Challenor needs some air.

If he's not careful, if he doesn't watch himself, if he doesn't listen to Doris's wise, wise words, he ends up cooped up, cooped up in the Mad House, stalking the corridors, pounding the corridors, looking for subordinates and other detectives to bother, to pester, to order about. He sees the young police constables who have worked for him, the same lads that did all that surveillance on Dirty Wilf and his two skin joints, and he sees them chatting, he sees them *nattering*, and it bothers Challenor, this twittering among these young lads, and he's sure that as he approaches the gaggles of young lads in uniform, he's sure that they shut their traps and look the other way, and he's not sure he likes this sense, this ominous and developing *weight*. He thinks there might be whisperings about the place. He's not sure, he can't be sure, but he does reckon there might well be some mutterings, some mutterings about him, around these corridors, these corridors he has taken to prowling while he waits for Lionel 'Curly' King to appear once again in his orbit.

He understands it though, to a point:

Uncle Harry Challenor, King of the Mad House –

Heavy lies the crown and whatnot.

And when this sense, this weight, gets a little hard to rationalise, when he feels a touch more bull-headed than he should, Challenor knows it's time for a stroll, for a *beat*, to, you know, put in a shift, do the old plod.

Time to let off a bit of steam. Once upon a merry morning, of course, he'd have done that down the boozer, but that won't work anymore. He's too old for a start. Christ, he thinks, a couple of brown ales at lunchtime and his head is heavier, nodding off in his chair. No, he's got business to attend to, he doesn't mess about, after all, Challenor. No, sir, he does not mess about.

Spring is in the air. No, hang about, Challenor thinks, that ain't right –

It's bloody January. Late January, but still.

Feels pretty mild for January, though. And there's a pleasing crispness to the air and a gorgeous, transparent light –

Transparent? That the word? It'll do.

Challenor stretches his legs onto Oxford Street.

He sets himself a brisk march, a decent, fair pace for a civvy setting, but still something of a clip. He can't help himself. When you need air, you need the blood to get about you, to, you know, what's the word, to *circulate*.

That expression: to clear your head. That quack of his down the river, that doctor who doesn't fancy him, reckons he's a bit off colour, in the bonce, him. Well, this quack has told Challenor that this expression – to clear your head – comes from the fact that a twenty-minute walk outside *actually clears your head*. The blood up there drains and changes, re-circulates. Funny business, medicine, funny old game this *biology* business, he thinks, the old human body, eh, what a palaver it all is.

There are tourists and shoppers, a light mid-morning throng. Challenor looks ahead from group to group, plots a course; he is, quite literally, he thinks, one step ahead of the rest.

He weaves and he shuffles, he feints and he bobs, he ducks and he drops a shoulder and he's in the clear, he's streaking away from the circling foreigners who examine maps and gasp as the buses grind and thunder their way down the road, on the wrong *side* of the road. And he's clear of Regent Street and it's a clear path east and then he pivots and starts right into old Soho, his Soho, down Poland Street and then a left and a right and he's on Berwick Street, and bugger me if he isn't looking straight at the back of young Lionel 'Curly' King's ample perm as young Mr King examines LPs in the window of a record shop –

'Allo 'allo, Challenor thinks and pulls himself back a few steps behind the corner of Broadwick Street.

Let's see what the Perm is up to, he thinks. Picked him for a music man, Challenor did. He'll be down the 2i's and the Marquee and all that –

He's got the locks for it, this rhythm and blues, Challenor thinks.

Challenor rifles his pockets, his wallet. He pulls a photo of a known Soho villain, a second-division porn operator. That'll do, he thinks.

Challenor hangs back as King decides against a purchase, then watches as he arrows down Broadwick –

Challenor does a right down Berwick, jogging now, then a left onto Peter Street.

He'll cut him off on Wardour Street –

Textbook ambush.

*

The morning after the RAF raid, the dust settles, literally settles, you can see it settling in front of your eyes as you stick your face out the window again, between the bars, to have a peer at the dust as it settles.

Your cell door opens. Here we go, you think, here we bloody go –

Payback time: for your cheek, your face.

You turn –

*

Challenor turns –

Lionel 'Curly' King turns. Lionel 'Curly' King sees Challenor. Lionel 'Curly' King turns again, sharp, and much quicker this time, and walks at some speed back the way he came.

Challenor sets off after him down Wardour Street.

Challenor is grinning. Thrill of the chase and whatnot.

Let's have you then, old son, Challenor thinks.

King slows down. To Challenor's eye it looks like King is reassessing his decision to scarper, to *flee*, as it were. There's time to reassess, certainly, Challenor will give him that.

King stops at steps into a doorway next to another record shop and examines a newspaper or periodical of some kind.

Gotcha, thinks Challenor. But also: clever boy.

*

You turn –

In front of you stands an officer. You can tell the lad's an officer both by his bearing – arrogant, upright, superior, though, you think, aren't all Krauts? – and by the stripes on his shoulder. SS, you suspect, proper little Aryan, touch of the Heydrich about him, the side-parted blonde hair, the ice in the blue of his eyes –

'Good morning,' the lad says. Clipped accent, but clear, crisp as a winter morning back home, Challenor thinks.

'Wotcha,' Challenor replies, and winks.

He's already up to his neck, he reckons, what with the previous night's japery and his general jovial approach to this torture and interrogation malarkey, so why not, eh, why not wind the buggers up even further? What's to lose, now, eh?

The officer smiles thinly. 'You're now going to tell me more about this SAS. Not the operation you've been on, we know all about that.'

'I expect you do. There's a bunch of derailed trains to testify to it. Yah?'

The officer gives you another thin smile. That 'yah' might have been a mistake, you think. He says, 'You're going to tell me all about this SAS, what it is, what is planned for it, where it came from, who is in it. Everything.'

'I don't know what you're talking about. What is this SAS? News to me, mate.'

Another thin smile. You think: he must be a cruel little bugger, or good with a blade, because if it comes to a set-to, he's a slender lad. Not a problem at all.

'I'm not wasting any more time, mine or yours. Speak.'

You shake your head. 'Nothing to say. And that's everything I know.'

The officer smiles, this time an actual, bona fide Jerry smile, he looks happy he does, quite pleased with the outcome. Hang about, you think, here we go again –

'OK, very well. This is what I expected, though not as I feared, I will be honest. You are of no use to us, you are a spy, and you will now, very shortly, be taken to the prisoner-of-war camp at L'Aquila where you will await execution. Is that clear?'

You nod. You smile. You grin –

*

'You recognise this man?' Challenor asks Lionel 'Curly' King, showing him the photo of the two-bob porn baron. As Challenor does this, he thinks that 'baron' might be too grand a word, really, and he allows himself a smirk, not quite a laugh, but he definitely acknowledges the humour in the whole scene.

King says, 'No, I don't.'

And King looks Challenor in the eye, but Challenor knows that there is fear in King's look, and Challenor thinks that it's not at all unsurprising given their last meeting.

Challenor's face is very close to King's face. Challenor can smell the scent on him, his face is that close to King's face. Spot of Old Spice, it is, the *scent*, though Challenor had King down as a more continental type, sophisticated, something a touch more *French*, you know, Challenor thinks, to go with the perm.

Challenor says nothing, but he is grinning like a bugger.

King's nervousness is exponential.

King says, 'My missus is waiting for me, I really should be going if there is nothing else I can help you with, Detective Challenor.'

Challenor grips King by the hair, by the back of his hair, grabs a fistful of his curly hair, his *mane*, and says, 'You don't start to behave, old son, and she will be waiting an awful lot longer.' He opens his fist, lets the hair escape, spring naturally back into place. 'You know what I mean?' he adds.

And Challenor smiles, winks and turns, turns on his heel, and is off, off towards Old Compton Street and Lucky Luke's trattoria as he seriously fancies a spot of Italian grub for lunch, and outside Mamma's farmhouse down Popoli way, down in Italia itself, he can't think of a better place than old Lucky Luke's.

*

Execution –
  What you hear though is:
  Prisoner-of-war camp –
  Which means:
  Company.
  A few of your own lads.
  A laugh or two, perhaps. A drink, even, maybe. Or two.
  What you hear is a bloody blessed relief, really, that's what it is, a bloody blessed relief, it really is.

Copper

My grandad was Old Bill.

'Your old grandad,' Tanky tells me, 'was a butcher's boy, then a plod, then a soldier, then ended up Superintendent of the Bournemouth police force. You should be proud, son.'

I was. I am.

'Here, have a look at this,' Tanky says.

He goes out into the hallway and comes back with a framed photo he's lifted from the wall.

It's my grandad and four other coppers, before the war, in full uniform, helmets included, treading water in the sea by the pier.

'The bobbing bobbies of Bournemouth!' Tanky says, delighted. 'That was the headline in the local paper, something like that, anyway. Bit different to my beat, I reckon, don't you, Bob?'

'Just a bit, yeah.'

Bob, I remember, was my grandad's nickname. God knows why.

'Bob the bobby!' Tanky says, laughing.

'Yeah, good one, Tanky,' my grandad says.

And my grandad knew it was very different, Tanky's beat.

In Bournemouth they had a system, the police and thieves, apparently. The cops and the robbers. My grandad and his lot would find cases of whisky, boxes of steaks and seafood tucked away behind certain bushes on certain roads. It was all fairly gentle. Equally though, my old grandad had no qualms about nudging a crook to jail with a bit of manipulated evidence, if the villain had crossed a line, of course. His point: we know they're guilty of something, so what's the harm of putting them inside for something else? The villains understood it, knew it was a fait accompli, and accepted the system.

Very different to Soho.

Six

'I've given you a chance. I could have found these in your pocket.'

It's now April, the 24th, and Challenor has moved on from the betting shops – they seemed to sort themselves out without too much bother; Challenor simply blocked all attempts to reopen them – but he has not forgotten about Lionel 'Curly' King and he is not happy about what he considers to be some serious face, some real *cheek* in King's avoiding him.

At least he assumes King has been avoiding him –

No one's seen the lad for months. Hiding out east, is the word, now he's not got a job in a Soho bookies. King likely reckons now it's all taken care of he can show his perm about town again. Word is, King's been buying records and been out in a few jazz clubs with his friend David Silver. One of Challenor's lookouts spotted them twenty minutes ago, having a coffee and a natter in some café or other at the end of Frith Street.

So Challenor has got hold of Police Constable Peter Warwick Jay and Detective Sergeant Kenneth Etheridge, and they've piled into a squad car, and they're now watching as King and Silver get into their own car on Old Compton and do a left onto Charing Cross Road.

There is not much going on. It is, Challenor thinks, helpfully quiet.

It's four in the morning, after all, he thinks, smiling.

King and Silver are not driving quickly.

'Pull up alongside him at the lights,' Challenor tells Police Constable Peter Warwick Jay.

'Right you are, guv.'

Challenor rubs his palms together – gleeful. *Here we bloody go*, he thinks.

Dish best served cold and all that. Young Lionel is not going to be too thrilled by the outcome of this evening's roistering.

Both cars stop at the lights. Challenor winds his window down and leans out. He raps his knuckles on the driver's window. 'Morning, Lionel. All right?'

King winds his window down. He's had a few, Challenor can see that. His face is a shade flushed, his eyes a touch bloodshot, they've narrowed a touch, his eyes.

Challenor points up ahead. 'Pull into Goslett Yard, and stop. And keep your hands on the wheel, son.'

King nods.

All five of them sit in the two cars and wait for the lights. King is giving his head quick little shakes, perhaps to focus, to think, perhaps to try and sober up. Silver, in the passenger seat, is twitchy, his eyes darting about; he seems, Challenor thinks, to be trying to check something on the back seat, but subtle like, not drawing attention to himself. Which, of course, Challenor realises, is exactly why he is drawing attention to himself. Jay is looking dead ahead, both hands on the steering wheel himself, nasty face on, serious. He knows the drill, Challenor thinks. Etheridge is cool, indifferent, slouched in the passenger seat, elbow resting on the door, right hand scratching at the side of his head –

He's here purely for numbers, and he knows it.

And Challenor? Challenor's grinning.

The lights change.

King turns left onto Goslett Yard.

Good boy.

———

*

You're put in a dormitory with a good lot of other lads, some of yours, some Italians, a few other sorts, Commonwealth, you know –

It is not palatial accommodation. There is not much space. And you don't have much time.

One thing you are certainly lacking is time.

Time. Time to work out how to check out, you think.

The dormitory is on the first floor. Officers are being kept below. At the back there is a small exercise yard. It is entirely surrounded by a double barricade of barbed wire fences and lookout towers, sentries. Facing your quarters is the prisoners' cookhouse, which serves black bread and watery cabbage soup through a hatch. This hatch is not big. It looks pretty well impenetrable.

You notice one other thing:

Italian women seem to come and go without ever being stopped or questioned.

What are they? Washerwomen?

There ain't too much time to figure it out.

*

Goslett Yard stinks of piss.

This is not a huge surprise given the time of night and the position of Goslett Yard. Perfect spot for a surreptitious slash, on an evening's tear-up, unable to hold your bladder's worth of brown ale. Perfect spot. Dark, no shops, empty doorways –

Challenor wrinkles his nose and grins. Bloody love it, he thinks, four in the morning and here we are down a piss-stinking alley about to reacquaint ourselves with an old chum who's about to reacquaint himself with what it means to be in trouble with the law, and, more specifically, the long arm of the law, the right fist of the law, the, quite possibly, fucking *forehead* of the law.

Challenor nods at Jay and Etheridge who move down the alley to King's car and open the doors and invite both Lionel King and David Silver to vacate the vehicle.

Challenor hangs back a touch, waits –

He can hear Jay telling the two lads to stand separate and to relax. He can hear Silver saying that he doesn't want to be searched in King's car. Etheridge looks over at Challenor. Challenor nods. Etheridge brings Silver over to the patrol car and opens the back door for him. Silver gets in. Etheridge follows and conducts a simple search of his person, then notes down Silver's account of the evening. The car window's open and Challenor hears Silver say, 'I must want my head examined, getting myself mixed up in all this.'

Challenor saunters over to Lionel 'Curly' King's car. He strolls over. He shimmies. He winks at Jay. He says to King, 'Now then, Lionel, you're going to let young Police Constable Peter Warwick Jay search your person, while I am going to search your car. I'd ask for your permission to do so, but I'm sure that knowing our relationship, our last meeting, our *previous*, as it were, you would happily grant it, so that to ask for it would constitute something of a waste of time.' Challenor pauses. 'Yours *and* mine. You in agreement, Lionel? Of course you are.'

King says nothing. King grimaces and raises his hands. King sways, touched a little by the old drink, he is, Challenor sees. It's late, after all.

Challenor leans into King's car. He pokes around for a little while. There is a cigarette case; there is a bag of LPs, jazz, by the look of them; there is a map; there is a jacket on the back seat; there is some miscellaneous detritus, food wrappers and so on; and there is a pillow, a cushion, under the front seat, the driver's seat.

Challenor ducks back out into Goslett Yard holding the cushion. He waves it at King. He thrusts it towards him. He *brandishes* it.

'Well, well, young man. Let's have a look in here,' Challenor says.

Challenor's hand snakes into his inside jacket pocket. He pulls out a fisherman's knife. He unclasps the blade. He plunges the blade into the cushion. He pulls down hard on the handle of the knife, yanking in a zigzag pattern. Feathers – white, small, frayed – float to the ground.

Challenor's satisfied with the hole he has dug into this now desiccated cushion, this pillaged pillow, and the thought of that makes him laugh, quietly, to himself. *Pillaged pillow*. And what with the feathers all about the place it looks like an Italian chicken coop after he's been in to find some supper, it does, down here in old piss-stinking Goslett Yard.

Challenor pokes his hand into the cushion. He rummages a little. He stops. He raises his eyebrows and smiles. He rummages a little more, for theatrical effect this time.

He has what he's looking for in his hand.

'Well, well,' he says.

He pauses. He pulls his hand from the cushion – triumphant.

And with a triumphant grin on his face.

He produces two detonators and shows them to King as a doctor might present a baby to a new mother.

King snaps into life, his drunkenness steadies itself. He says, 'Don't look any further, detective. There's no jelly here. You could score all this down to aggravation. We're unlucky, that's all. That's someone else's gear.'

Challenor shakes his head, still grinning. He says, 'I've two detonators here, my old darling. You're in the frame for those bookies. You're nicked.' He pauses. He steps over to Lionel 'Curly' King. He nods at Police Constable Peter Warwick Jay, who steps away. Challenor speaks fast, sinister, right into Lionel 'Curly' King's scared little face. He says, 'I've given you a chance, lad. I could have found these in your pockets.'

*

'You are having a fucking laugh, old son!'

And there are peals of laughter. There are hoots of laughter. The whole dormitory is roaring, now, with laughter.

And you're laughing too.

'So, what you're telling, us, young man, what you're fucking trying to tell us, is that you, SAS, a thing we've never really heard of, you know, officially, that you, you're SAS, whatever the fuck it is, you are going to escape this prisoner-of-war camp, or you'll get fucking executed, you're going to escape this place, this relatively comfortable place to spend the fucking war, you're going to escape it by walking out – '

The laughter is echoing. The laughter is ringing out –

' – by walking out, walking out in broad fucking daylight, walking out dressed as a fucking washerwoman!'

By this time, the laughter is possibly attracting some attention –

You, grinning, trying not to, trying to shush your lads, who aren't half taking the bloody piss –

'A fucking washerwoman! Mate, you are a genius. A madman, oh absolutely, but quite possibly a bona fide genius.'

This lad raises a finger and everyone else shuts up.

He smiles, very broadly. 'How can we bloody well help?'

*

While Lionel 'Curly' King is in custody, his home address is searched, and Challenor is pleased that the young constables conducting the search have come across a forged driving licence.

Challenor's got Lionel 'Curly' King in his office now and is quite enjoying sharing the news of this discovery.

Radio's on.

The news ends and a song begins to play and Challenor's

ears prick up and his mouth twitches in pleasure.

And the opening of 'He's So Fine' by The Chiffons kicks in, with its doo-lang, doo-lang backing vocal and Challenor cackles with laughter.

'Oh, I like this one,' he says. 'I love a doo-wop, soul combo. Love a girl group that swings and sways like these. Have a listen, son. It's rather an apt 45, lyrics wise.'

King scowls. King crosses his arms. King seems, actively, to be trying to *not* listen, if that's at all possible, Challenor thinks.

If he were a kid, he'd have his hands over his ears.

Challenor leans across the desk and mouth the words of the song at young Lionel as it plays. There are a couple of quite pertinent lyrics, Challenor thinks, grinning, all about a handsome boy and his wavy hair, how she wishes he were hers.

Challenor leans back in his chair and doesn't half laugh. 'Wavy hair, eh? Handsome man, wavy hair and all that. Good lyrics, aren't they, Lionel? Remind you of anyone?'

The song plays on and switches key. The backing vocal chimes, the rhythm swings and sways.

'We'll just enjoy the rest of it, shall we?' Challenor says.

They sit and say nothing. The song lasts a minute or so more.

Challenor's lips are pursed, he's smiling, humming, nodding his head, tapping his foot.

'Yeah, it's a cracker this one,' he says, as the song ends.

King is stony-faced.

'Now then, Lionel, about this moody driving licence. I can't see it helping you, old son. Any thoughts?'

King nods. 'Yeah,' he says. 'And it's Irish, I swear, God's honest. OK?'

Challenor raises an eyebrow.

King continues: 'It was for someone else. This nutter was going to blast a certain speiler, right. He was going to use a nicked car with a dummy licence in case he got a pull. All I had to do was supply the necessary. The funny part about it all is that I didn't even get the dets. I was just born unlucky.' King breathes out, really *sighs*. 'And that's straight up, Harry. I swear.'

Challenor nods. He looks at King for a few moments. King does not enjoy these few moments, Challenor can see that. This is a little web, Challenor thinks, and wonders quite what King *will* admit to, to, you know, free himself of some greater charge.

Challenor considers this and considers what to say next. He thinks of The Chiffons and the handsome man with the wavy hair.

Challenor smiles – wide.

'Well,' he says.

And then, breaking into song, Challenor sings from the second verse, adding the doo-lang, doo-langs himself. She don't know how she's going to do it, Challenor's singing, but she will certainly make this handsome man hers.

*

Here's how they can help:

A long old pair of black woollen socks. Rags and cloth, blankets and sheets. You nod –

'Good lads,' you tell them.

Then everyone in the dormitory is scratching around for any needles and thread, and there are a surprising number of them. And then, the more skilful of the lads help you to sew up one of the lice-ridden blankets into a rather nice-looking skirt.

Your first lad says, roaring, 'Eh, lads, nice bit of skirt!'

And there is more laughter. You had no idea what devilry you were going to stir up in this prisoner-of-war, awaiting-execution camp you'd been plonked into.

Then you're sat on the edge of a bed, and a couple of the even more skilful lads give you a shave with the sharpest blade they can find.

It feels fucking fantastic!

But it might not be quite enough, so a couple of the less skilful lads rub some of the white plaster from the walls all over your face, all over your grinning mug, your handsome, grinning mug, transformed into a fairly ugly-looking Italian peasant woman, at least that's the bloody plan –

You lie down to get a little rest, try to sleep.

You are pretty fucking far from confident. You have travelled hundreds of miles. You have been lucky beyond your wildest imagination. You have blown apart trains in the name of your country, in a fight against an evil empire. You realise how that sounds, but it is simply true. You have trained and trained and trained to become a brutal killing machine, a man of stealth and wit and imagination. You have been captured and tortured, beaten, starved and tortured, beaten, starved and tortured because of your training, because of what you have done in the name of your country in this fight against this evil empire, and because of this, you are to be put to death, put down like a dog, executed. Executed. What a fucking word, eh? Executed.

And how are you going to use your training and your stealth and your wit and your imagination to avoid this fate?

You're going to crawl through a serving hatch, hitching up your bloody lice-ridden skirt as you do it, and then walk calmly past guards and sentries dressed as a woman with white plaster on her face.

What a wally you are.

There's no fucking way.

You don't sleep. This is so hare-brained as to be a fucking joke –

And that's when you smile.

What else can it be? This is a game, all right, my old son.

He who has nothing has no fear of death.

*

20th June 1963 –

Challenor is sitting in his office when he gets the news.

The charges:

Receiving stolen detonators, possessing detonators with intent to cause malicious damage to a building by explosion, and conspiracy to cause malicious damage to a building –

Convicted and sent down:

Silver for six months.

King? A two stretch for young Lionel. Two solid years.

Challenor smiles – wolfish. He wonders how Lionel will maintain his stylish demeanour, his rakish allure, inside, inside with those animals; maintain his perm, in short, in a land where a dandyish sense is not always best appreciated.

Challenor laughs. Poor old Lionel and his perm –

He wonders if he'll go down Brixton, meet up with old Oliva and his mob –

What a fucking result, eh?

*

Next morning –

The hatch is open and the guard collecting the rations has gone. Time for you to move. You dress in your skirt and shawl and rub more plaster on your cheeks.

Christ, you think, most old Italian peasant birds don't look too clever after that life of hard work, but they're fucking Cinderella compared to you.

Down to the exercise yard, wrapped up in a great coat.

The lads mill around you, shuffle as a group, in a circle, you in the middle, towards the hatch –

You peer through it: the corridor that leads to a door that leads to the outside of the main building is empty.

Here we fucking go, you say.

Three of the lads lift you up, gather your skirt and heave you through the hatch.

'Best of luck, Tanky,' you hear.

'Who dares wins,' you whisper back.

And then, again, you're on your own.

*

Challenor is sauntering about West End Central. He's got his hands in his pockets. He's whistling. He's waltzing about in finest seafaring style, not a care, oh no, son, not a care in the world, not a care in the old world.

He's top dog, top boy, top banana. King Challenor rules –

King Challenor rules the roost, all right. Oh yes, he certainly does, King Challenor. The accolades are pouring in. Brass is happy. The Soho sewer is running cleaner. There are a few more faces inside. And there is a good deal less criminal activity, it appears, on the streets, on Challenor's streets, on King Challenor's streets.

And if his methods are a little unorthodox, if he doesn't exactly play by the rules, doesn't always do things *by the book*, well, who cares. A Maurice Harding, a very well-respected CID, a man who does not suffer fools, not a man to heap praise, not an effusive man, has been quoted as saying: 'I like Challenor. He's nicking the right people at the right time.'

Challenor thinks about this quote and it helps him to ignore the whispers of his so-called, self-proclaimed immunity to censure.

Challenor's heard that he reckons he's untouchable, invincible. That his war record, that what he did in Italy and France means that no one will ever get the better of him.

Heavy lies the crown, old son.

Shrug all that off.

He's also heard something else, might be the biggest compliment he's ever had.

He's heard that the Twins are offering a grand to anyone without a criminal record who will let Challenor stitch them up, and then turn the tables on him, bringing about his downfall.

Yeah, Challenor's heard this. Krays are behind it, so they say, but it's a joint effort, apparently.

The Soho criminal fraternity are not happy.

The Krays can fuck off, Challenor thinks, smiling. He's only chased Reggie down Shaftesbury Avenue not that long ago, after all.

He escorted the pair of them back to East London on another night. They were civil enough about it, that evening.

And most recently, early summer, 1963, Challenor had rung his old contact David Parkinson to see if they were in a club in Gerrard Street.

And they certainly were.

But by the time Challenor arrived, they'd legged it.

Someone in the rubber-heeled squad must have had a word.

*

You shuffle down the corridor. The corridor feels endless. You want to hurry, but you know you mustn't. The corridor goes on and on –

The corridor is lined by offices. A door opens –

You shuffle on, trying not to look at the Jerry orderly who bustles past, weighed down by a folder of documents.

He doesn't even notice you.

Christ, you think. What the hell are you doing?

You reach the end of the corridor, the end of this endless corridor, and at the end of this endless corridor, there is a door.

You push the door at the end of this endless corridor, you push it and it opens –

It opens and you're outside the main building, with one more obstacle to pass –

The perimeter fence gate, thirty yards away, guarded by two soldiers.

You breathe. You breathe in and out. You tighten the shawl around your shoulders. You do not look at the rifles that the soldiers carry.

You have walked three hundred miles since landing in Italy, on that cool, dark, blue, black night, in Italy, in a tree, somewhere in northern Italy –

But these thirty yards are further than this, longer than the three hundred miles you have walked across this beautiful country, Italy.

You believe that your average German is an arrogant sod. And you're banking on it now. They didn't pick you at the church on Christmas Eve, after all?

You're trying to reassure yourself. You take one step, then another. One more step, then another step. You shuffle on, your shawl wrapped tight, your blanket skirt slipping –

No! It's not the skirt, it's your long johns, your long johns that are slipping!

You wriggle and pull as you walk, you keep walking, you mustn't stop –

Fifteen yards.

Your voice echoes in your head: this is too good to last.

Five yards. And a couple more steps, and you're there, you're at the gate and you're turning the handle, and, thank Christ, you were right about your average German, there's no way on God's earth either of these fuckers is going to help an old Italian peasant woman, no way they're going to open the door and stand aside for an ugly, old Italian peasant woman –

And you're through.

And your long johns have just about stayed up.

And you're walking down the road, ambling down the road, shuffling down the road and an old man – an ancient *man – clatters by in a donkey-drawn cart and he invites you to hop in and you're away –*

And you get your bearings and you know that in not too long, the beatings and hunger behind you, you'll be back with Mamma and the others at the Eliseio farm.

Who dares wins.

*

Thing is, Challenor's also hearing that the unhappy Soho criminal fraternity have their own nickname for him –

King Cunt.

Bent

After Italy came France in August 1944, and if the Italian job made Tanky, then Operation Wallace – as the behind-the-lines jaunt across north-western France from Orleans to Belfort, in the forest of Châtillon, just north of Dijon was known – made 2SAS.

Major Roy Farran led twenty jeeps and sixty men. They were parachuted in and just got on with it. The goal: cause a bit of chaos, post-D-Day, to facilitate the advance of the American Third Army. Chaos meaning blow shit up and fuck up a few Jerries while they were at it. All a bit *Boys' Own*, I know, but why not? It worked, after all.

This was also my grandad's operation. He and Tanky had first met on training, then they were together on the submarine on Operation Marigold off the coast of Sardinia.

And it made him, I reckon. Hard not to be formed by an experience like that.

I wear his engagement ring to this day. It saved his life during Operation Wallace. His jeep tore around a corner and there was a Jerry roadblock. They slammed on the brakes and reversed back when the Krauts opened up. One of the lads tumbled out of the jeep and got one in the neck. My grandad grabbed the roll bar, his ring caught, and he clung on and stayed in. Next day, they blew that roadblock back to wherever it came from.

The ring lasted another fifty years, despite the thin, bent band caused by that moment of purchase. After my grandad died, I got the ring. I wore it for six months and then it snapped in a pocket when I was playing pool in the pub. My grandmother laughed when I told her. I got it fixed easily enough and put it straight back on.

Major Farran wrote a book called *Winged Dagger* and there is a hefty chapter on Operation Wallace. My grandad is mentioned several times. During the battle of Châtillon, a dozen SAS killed a hundred Germans, wounded many more, and destroyed nine trucks, four cars and a motorcycle.

Farran is an entertaining writer.

> I was astonished to see a German machine-gun post on each side, facing outwards… I could not think what to do, so we sat in a garden and waited. Lieutenant Pinci begged a bottle of wine, bread and cheese from a French cottage, so we had lunch.
>
> I tossed up which German we should shoot in the back and it turned out to be the left-hand one. Sergeant Young took careful aim through his carbine and when I gave the word, he pulled the trigger.

Sergeant Young: that's my grandad. He was certainly a marksman. At the end of the war, when they were up in Norway, basically hanging out, he heard my grandma was pregnant with my aunt. Farran let him go and he hitched a lift with a fishing boat that was crossing the North Sea. Problem was, he realised, there was a shit-tonne of mines all about the place and the skipper wasn't exactly overly cautious in his approach to navigation, or steering. Cavalier doesn't cover it. So my grandad stayed up for two days and two nights at the front of the boat with his trusty carbine, picking them off, any mines that popped up in the way.

And he got home in time to see Auntie Liz born.

Why am I telling you all this?

Because I'm proud of my grandad, immensely proud of what he did, of how he lived his life. My mum always says that when they went camping in the summers, down in France or Spain, after the war, he was always the first to talk to any German holidaymakers. Something he understood: most of them were just young lads, like he was, like Tanky was, like Big Jim Mackie was, like Tojo was, like Cas Carpenter was, like Freddie Baines and Will Fyffe, like Pouch Maybury and 'Umbriago', like Larry Brownlee and Paddy McCann, like Sammy Harrison and Jake Manders, younger lads, all of them, than I am now – much younger. Operation Wallace lasted a month, a month behind the lines, a month when around every corner it was likely a German machine post was waiting to rip you apart, and the total number of trucks they blew up was something like ninety-five.

The operation was, in Tanky's words, a sophisticated form of licensed mugging.

So, yeah, I'm proud of my grandad and everything he did. One good little story: my mum's first husband was a conscientious objector. I know, right? Anyway, she decided that the best time for him to meet her old man was at an SAS reunion. Sense of humour on her, my mum. So there's this handsome little ratty man scurrying about, all confident, apparently, chatty and fun, meeting all this SAS mob, and not a single one of them was anything other than friendly, welcoming, understanding of this lad's position, his decision to conscientiously object to National Service. And you know why? Because none of them would wish what they did on anyone. They did what they did so there would be no war.

I'm proud of my grandad, and there's barely a day when I don't wish I could say it. I was a kid when he died. I didn't know what it meant, to be proud. I often wonder if he'd be proud of me, of the man I've become.

I'm proud of everything he did, proud of how he lived his life.

But I'm not sure quite how Tanky lived his life –

And I'm definitely not proud of everything he ever did.

Seven

'The biggest brick for the biggest boy!'
July 11th, 1963

Challenor is steaming. Challenor is furious. Challenor is not a happy chap.

He's right in the thick of an investigation into a 'near beer' and clip-joint establishment on Frith Street called the Boulevard club. He loves the old 'near beer' terminology: a place that waters down its lager to such an extent it doesn't need a licence for booze. Clip joint is not such a pleasant description of what that entails. He's never quite worked it out: *clip*? You promise a punter a bird, a lady of the night, and off you go to her rooms, and instead of a leg over, you have all the cash liberated from your pocket.

Clipped.

And he's making progress, too. He's had Patricia 'Fat Pat' Hawkins in, the Madame of the operation, and 'Black' Harold Padmore, a strapping Barbadian who used to be a cricketer but now only bowls wrong 'uns. Yeah, he's making progress. There's been more than a few punters, a few marks, who've left the Boulevard's upstairs rooms after feeling a touch of 'Black' Harold's blade.

So, Challenor is furious to have this little job interrupted.

He knows he went a bit far with Fat Pat, shouldn't have touched her. 'May God forgive you,' she'd said. 'He probably won't,' Challenor had replied. And it wasn't really on to be singing that old song by Danny

Kaye and The Andrews Sisters, 'Bongo, bongo, bongo, I don't want to leave the Congo' as he laid into old Harold. He may have gone a bit far there. Not sure they got the joke; not sure they understood the *psychology* behind this particular witness intimidation. PC Robb looked a bit shocked by it, too, Challenor thinks. 'Take the black bastard out of my sight,' Challenor told him, after he'd handed Padmore a lively tune-up. 'I wish I lived in South Africa,' Challenor had said. 'I'd have a spade for breakfast every morning.' No, old PC Robb didn't look too sure about that remark, Challenor thinks.

Yeah, maybe I went a bit far, he concedes.

On the other hand, justice prevailed, he thinks, when push came to shove. He got the confession, didn't he?

End of the day, Challenor knows which way the court will vote when it comes to the testimonies, which way the wind blows: he is white, after all. And Padmore's a known face, so Brass is quite happy for him to take a kicking, as one of the more 'louche' elements of old Soho. And Challenor's a highly respected detective, of course, the Scourge of Soho, war hero, King Challenor.

King Cunt.

Challenor had a word with Doris after that. He told her: 'If anyone tells you I'm having a breakdown, you mustn't worry about it, it's all part of a plan.'

But this plan is being interrupted by a state fucking visit, from fucking Queen Frederika of Greece, Elizabeth II's own third cousin, the great-granddaughter of Queen Victoria and Kaiser Wilhelm II, and who, growing up in Germany, was a fully fledged member of the Hitler Youth in the 1930s.

That might be enough, but that's not why Challenor is incandescent with a sort of low-level rage, a nagging wrath.

No, he's fed up because a whole mob of lefties and anarchists and the old Committee of 100 have been protesting outside Claridge's on Brook Street – where the gorgeous Greek Queen is parking her royal backside – for the last couple of days, and just the evening before, Challenor tended to the wounds of Police Inspector George Brooks, who had been hit slap-bang in the face by a brick thrown by one of these so-called political protestors, as he was on duty, just doing his job, outside Claridge's itself.

Challenor's had it with this lefty mob. And he's after them.

Soho, after all, and the odd bit of posh Mayfair, is, lest any cunt forget, his kingdom.

*

Challenor grabs Police Constable David John Oakey, one of the aides to CID, and tells him: 'Get your glad rags on, young man, we're going out.'

Challenor's heard that there are going to be around fifteen hundred officers out on the streets around Claridge's tonight. Officers of all rank, all file, all sorts out, some sympathisers with the protestors, others out to break heads –

Challenor knows what he fancies:

A few collars felt. Some arrests.

He likes to keep his arrest rate up, does Challenor. Always has. There was a time, back in Croydon, on his first beat, he'd do that by nicking the homeless. It was a winner: they were happy as they got a bed and a bit of shelter for the night –

And Challenor made his numbers.

'Come on, son,' Challenor says to Oakey, as he shoulders the front door of West End Central. They push up Bond Street, do a left onto Avery Row, and just ahead, on Brook Street, there is a sizeable crowd intent, it appears, on mischief. It is just after eight o'clock in the evening. It is a balmy evening. The light is gorgeous, Challenor thinks, a real fat glow to it, a definite *balm*, a right old summer's night for trouble.

'It looks like a naughty group, does it not, David?'

Oakey nods. 'What's the brief, guv?'

Challenor grins. 'We are after any chaps with rocks and bricks and other makeshift offensive weapons. You know the drill.'

Oakey nods again. He does know the drill. It's why Challenor strong-armed him out the door for himself.

Brook Street is heaving. It's a real mass of bodies, all swaying, moving this way and that, like a football crowd, or a Rolling Stones show, Challenor thinks. Fewer tarts, mind.

There are banners. One says: 'Lambrakis R.I.P'

Challenor recognises the name. It's why they're here, really. A Greek political activist killed in fairly mysterious – and by mysterious, Challenor means *very dodgy* – circumstances.

He nods at the banner. 'Any excuse for a meet, eh, David?'

Oakey nods once more. They peer about them, try and get some purchase on what sort of a crowd they're dealing with here.

'Keep a close eye on that banner, David,' Challenor says.

Challenor is wearing a long coat with deep pockets, and his old Tank Corps beret –

Tanky's about.

He figured he'd fit in with all the anarchists and the militants in a sort of faux-military get-up.

Though what do they know, of course, these anarchists and militants, about real conflict?

Fuck all. Throwing bricks mob-handed? Wankers.

Challenor can see uniformed officers mixing it up in the fray. He can see the odd plainclothes jostle the less-savoury-looking elements.

The air is thick with promise.

It's one of those nights, Challenor thinks. His eyes narrow as he snakes this way and that. The air is, in fact, thick with the smell of jazz cigarettes, Challenor thinks. Not his remit.

Challenor and Oakey worm through the crowds. It is a per-tinent fucking contrast, the towers flanking a marching band of anti-royalists. Or pro-democrats. These days it's all so black and white it's hard to tell the difference, know where the, you know, know where the ideological lines are drawn and that.

Challenor imposes his will on the crowd, the *mass*. Triumph of it, you know, triumph of the will, and all that, he thinks. He's going to get where he needs to go through sheer fucking *character*. Didn't work too well with those rubber dinghies though, he remembers. But, you know, as they say, you win some –

You win some more.

He's cock of the walk, Challenor. Swaggering like a broad-shouldered, thick-set, bull-necked Prince among thieves.

No, King. King –

King Cunt. Own *that*, my son.

'You still got that banner in your sight, David?' Challenor asks.

Oakey nods.

Either way. Challenor knows *exactly* where the Lambrakis R.I.P banner is. He's clocked it halfway down Brook Street and he's after it.

Then: movement –

Close by.

Oakey's got some obviously hateful, dago-looking kid by the neck –

Two uniforms are over, sharpish.

Oakey's saying to the uniforms: 'Brick. In his hand. Nick him. Offensive weapon. Take him down the Mad House.'

Good lad.

There's the first. Good start to the night's festivities. Challenor pats Police Constable David John Oakey on the shoulder.

Oakey grins.

Good lad.

Challenor grins. And we're off, he thinks.

*

Turns out there are two other lads along with the one Oakey pulled, then Challenor and Oakey head down Brook Street until it reaches Gilbert Street, swerving the thick, seething middle of the crowd, pavement-hopping and moving swiftly, skipping even, at times, hopping, skipping and jumping to nip in and out of this crowd, this mass, this writing, seething mass, this angry mass –

And they are angry, this mob.

Eyes peeled.

'What we're looking for, boy, is more stones,' Challenor says. 'Stones, bricks, cement – all that. At some point, these fuckers are going to want to throw something at something, you know what I mean?'

Oakey nods.

'And the way we're going to find these stones and rocks and bits of brick and so on, is to find people – men, I suspect, in the main – wearing the type of jacket which has the type of pockets that might accommodate these stones and rocks and bricks.'

Challenor is firing these words out of the side of his mouth like a volley of machine-gun fire, or a mortar launch or something like that. And Oakey is doing his best to keep up, both with Challenor's feet – which are deceptively quick for such a pugnacious fellow – and Challenor's words, which are, Challenor realises, being fired out of his mouth.

'And that, David, is exactly why I am wearing this jacket.'

Oakey nods.

'I fit in. We can get closer to them.' He gestures with his chin, nods to the right-hand side of the street. 'Here we go,' he says. 'Here we fucking go, follow me.'

And Challenor arrows in on a group of five gentleman dressed in flat caps and work coats, and one of them goes to put his hand in his pocket and –

Challenor's on him in a flash –

Two quick steps, then a solid, definitive lunge, a proper *tackle* –

With his forearm he's pinned him against the wall. At the same time, he knocks the flat cap from his head and pulls the work coat down over his arms to trap them and hold him in place.

'Stay still, young man. You're nicked.'

Challenor puts his face very close to the face of this young man, who snarls back at him, like a dog, afraid, but showing his teeth with it, not shirking this unexpected challenge.

'What for?' says the snarling, braying young man.

The crowd has thinned slightly where they are, filtered off with the minor commotion of Challenor's move, his launch, his *assault*, the crowd ebbing and flowing around them like they were rocks in a river.

'You reached into your pocket for a rock, or brick, or stone, which I have no doubt you intended to throw, though, to be clear, intent to throw or hurl or *launch* is irrelevant. Possession of an offensive weapon. Possession. Got it?'

'I was reaching into my pocket for my cigarettes.'

Challenor leans closer still, angles his face right into this young man's face.

'Hold tight. We'll see.'

Oakey appears with four uniforms and two other young, angry, snarling men, both handcuffed.

'Take him in,' Challenor says. 'He was reaching for this.'

Challenor hands one of the uniforms a chunky segment of house brick.

The young man struggles. 'That's not mine, mate. That's a plant.' He looks at the uniforms. 'I ain't going anywhere with you lot.'

Challenor laughs. 'You've got no choice, my darling. Stick them all in the meat wagon, lads,' he says to the uniforms.

The snarling, braying man is cuffed.

Challenor smiles at Oakey.

Oakey nods.

Challenor says, 'That's seven nil then, eh?'

Oakey nods.

*

It's been a busy hour. It needs to get busier. Challenor does not mess about. Challenor is not going to mess about with these anarchists and militants and flag-burning types who'll boo the Queen and have a go at the very people paid to protect them, paid, in fact, *by* them to protect *them*, if, you know, these buggers even *pay* their taxes.

Time to find that banner.

Back down Brook Street, up Davies Street, along Davies Mews, down South Molton Lane. Eyes at street level. Nothing to see. Shops closed.

There.

Challenor nods at the banner and Oakey quickens his pace.

There are two flags flanking the banner, two CND flags flanking the Lambrakis R.I.P banner, and this collection of flags and banner make it very clear of the political leanings of this group.

The CND flags are being carried by two women, young women with short hair, young women with short hair in clipped style held in place by their red berets, two young women who are considerably younger than the man in between them with the banner. Considerably younger. If Challenor didn't know better, if Challenor weren't such a man of the world, he might guess that this was a professor at the LSE with two of his most promising students, showing them the significance and consequence of direct action in political life.

But Challenor does know better, and to Challenor's worldly eye it looks like what it is: a creep with two tarts. No doubt the creep is the leader of some minor political organisation – commie or anarchist, Challenor would bet – and these two considerably younger women are under his spell in some important, coming-of-age, coming-of-political-consciousness way, but still, it's a creep with two tarts. Shamans the world over helping young women find bloody God, or spiritual fervour, or political activism, or whatever – and then helping them find themselves on their backs with a creepy Shaman on top, slobbering all over them.

Yeah, Challenor doesn't fancy this banner lad much. Not at all, in fact.

Challenor raises his hand and Oakey stops.

The banner and the CND flags drift past them.

Challenor indicates with his hands that they should follow, but either side.

They fall in step. The crowd ebbs. Their steps become fewer. They stop.

Challenor leans across one of the young women and grabs banner lad by the lapel with his right hand.

He yanks him backwards.

He grabs his throat with his left hand and squeezes his windpipe.

He pushes him across South Molton Lane and into a shop doorway.

He looks back and sees Oakey encouraging the young women to move on, nothing to see and all that.

Challenor, through half-shut, piercing eyes, with a thin, self-consciously nasty smile sliced across his face as if with a straight razor, takes a good look at this lad, this older lad, in his scruffy blazer and fisherman's hairy jumper, with his beard and the faint twirl in his moustache, in his corduroy trousers rolled up to show off his working man's boots, with his Lenin cap and glasses, and says,

'You're fucking nicked, my old beauty.'

———

*

Banner lad's name is Donald Rooum.

He was born in Bradford in 1928. He was an anarchist, then a conscientious objector, then did his National Service, then studied commercial design, then worked as a layout artist, then a typographer, then a cartoonist and lecturer. He has fathered four children.

He is also a member of the National Council for Civil Liberties.

Challenor gets all this information while Rooum is detained upstairs.

Here we fucking go.

Challenor tears through his office door and jumps the stairs –

What are you going to do about it?

Challenor slams open the detention room door, which bounces back off the wall at him, so he kicks at it, grabs at it, wrenches it off its hinges and throws it down on the floor, kicks at it again, clatters it against the far wall.

Rooum is not bothered much by this show of rage, of wrath, Challenor thinks.

Here we fucking go then.

'Boo the Queen, would you?' Challenor asks.

'No, not at all,' Rooum replies.

Challenor, with his right palm, hits Rooum's left ear, right on the lug.

'You said "down with the monarchy". Why?'

'I'd say that was clear, wouldn't you?'

Challenor, with his right palm, hits Rooum's left ear again, square on, right on the lug, directly over the old ear hole.

'You don't like where you live, where you're from?'

'I believe in democracy and fairness and a system of government that – '

Challenor, with his right palm, hits Rooum's left ear again, square on, right on the lug, directly over the old ear hole, and at the same time, with the edge of his left palm, chops down on Rooum's neck.

Rooum looks dazed.

'What were you doing at the demonstration?'

'I was protesting at a state visit by a representative of a repressive government.'

'And why your antipathy towards the police, boy?'

'They shouldn't push us around like that.'

Challenor, this time with his right palm closed around the chunky segment of a house brick that is wrapped in brown paper, hits Rooum's left ear, square on, right on the lug, directly over the old ear hole.

Rooum staggers. Blood trickles from his ear.

'Right,' Challenor says. He unwraps the brick from the brown paper. 'There you are, my old beauty. This is yours. The biggest brick for the biggest boy.'

He places the chunky segment of brick on the evidence table along with Rooum's other possessions.

Challenor continues. 'Carrying an offensive weapon. You can get two years for that. Give those young tarts of yours a bit of time to grow up. Think they'll visit?'

Rooum blinks. Rooum gags. Rooum vomits.

Challenor hesitates –

The Trial

June 4th, 1964
The Old Bailey

Challenor sits. Challenor sits and waits, sits and waits for the verdict.

Today's the day.

It is, for Challenor at least, for Challenor and three other more junior officers, aides, in fact, to CID, Challenor's boys, you might call them, Battes and Goldsmith and Oakey, it is, for them, quite literally, Judgement Day.

The charge:

Corruption.

Mr Justice Lawton is speaking. He is talking about Chief Superintendent John 'Four day Johnny' du Rose, so called for his efficient and effective approach to solving crimes.

Challenor is listening to what Mr Justice Lawton is saying, but he is not really sure about how it makes him feel.

'…Chief Superintendent du Rose, I would be very grateful if you would bring to the attention of the Commissioner my grave disturbance at the fact that Detective Sergeant Challenor was on duty at all on 11th July 1963. On the evidence which I heard from the doctors when he was arraigned, it seems likely that he had been mentally unbalanced for some time, and the evidence which I heard from Superintendent Burdett in the case has worried me a great deal. It seems to me the matter ought to be looked into further.'

Challenor sits. Challenor waits. Challenor sits and waits and thinks about this idea, this further investigation, of it being 'looked into'.

Challenor fingers again the piece of paper he has in his pocket.

If you can wait and not be tired by waiting,

Or being lied about, don't deal in lies.

Verdicts are in.

Verdict One –

The three junior officers, the three aides, the three boys, Challenor's boys, Battes, Goldsmith and Oakey:

Guilty

Battes gets three years. Goldsmith and Oakey four each.

Challenor's head swims. His head dives. His head *sinks*.

Verdict Two –

Detective Sergeant Harold 'Uncle Harry' 'Tanky' Challenor, on the charge of corruption, relating specifically to events of the evening of July 11th, 1963:

Unfit to Plead

Bibliography

This is a work of fiction based on fact. Some of the stories and incidents related are apocryphal; some of them have been passed down my family, in the oral tradition. Below is a list of sources I consulted in the writing of this novel; a list of quoted material follows. The images and text from the 'blue photo album' are from my grandfather's personal archive. I visited the Camden Local Studies and Archives Centre in the Holborn Library for a visual impression of the area around Theobalds Road and Bloomsbury in the early 1960s. I have frequented the pubs and clubs referenced in their more recent iterations.

Non-fiction

Ackroyd, Peter, *London: The Concise Biography*, (Vintage, 2012)

Beevor, Antony, *The Second World War*, (Weidenfeld and Nicolson, 2014)

Challenor, Harold, with Alfred Draper, *Tanky Challenor: SAS and the Met,* (Leo Cooper, 1990)

Farran, Roy, *Winged Dagger: Adventures on Special Service,* (Cassell Military Classics, 1998)

Gilbert, Martin, *The Second World War: A Complete History*, (Weidenfeld and Nicolson, 2009)

Grigg, Mary, *The Challenor Case,* (Penguin Books, 1965)

James, A. E., *Report of Inquiry, CMND. 2735*, HMSO, 1965

Kirby, Dick, *The Scourge of Soho: The controversial career of SAS hero Detective Sergeant Harry Challenor,* (Pen & Sword True Crime, 2013)

Macintyre, Ben, *SAS Rogue Heroes*, (Viking, 2016)

Morton, James, *Bent Coppers: A survey of police corruption*, (Warner Books, 1994)

Warner, Philip, *The Special Air Service*, (edition commissioned by SAS
    Regimental Association, bound by Sangorski & Sutcliffe, 1973;
    originally published by William Kimber & Co, 1971)
Willetts, Paul, *Members Only*, (Serpent's Tail, 2010)

Fiction
Arnott, Jake, *The Long Firm Trilogy*, (Sceptre, 2005)
Toms, Bernard, *The Strange Affair*, (Panther Books, 1968)
Unsworth, Cathi, *Bad Penny Blues*, (Serpent's Tail, 2009)

Plays
Butterworth, Jez, *Mojo*, (Nick Hern Books, 2013)
Orton, Joe, *Loot*, (Bloomsbury Methuen Drama, 2013)

Films
Night and the City, Jules Dassin, 1950
Peeping Tom, Michael Powell, 1966
Performance, Donald Cammell & Nicholas Roeg, 1970
Street of Shadows, Richard Vernon, 1953
The Long Good Friday, John Mackenzie, 1980
The Small World of Sammy Lee, Ken Hughes, 1963
Victim, Basil Dearden, 1961
Where has poor Mickey gone?, Gerry Levy, 1964

Radio
Bent Coppers, Jake Arnott, Archive on 4, BBC Radio 4, 2019

Journalism
Interview with Joseph Francis Oliva, first published in the *Daily Sketch*
    newspaper, 30 June 1959

Notes

Challenor's career was controversial; there were several inquiries held into his conduct. Excerpts from the James Inquiry, 1965, and court proceedings in the trials of Pedrini et al, King etc, have appeared in a number of non-fiction texts included in my bibliography. Here follow instances where I too have used or adapted them, with references to these texts, and other quoted material. Challenor's memoir – *Tanky Challenor: SAS and the Met* – was especially helpful in the writing of the scenes set in Italy; my grandfather's experiences, too, were invaluable in these sections.

Page 2
If you can wait and not be tired by waiting,
Or being lied about, don't deal in lies. From 'If' by Rudyard Kipling

Page 7
'A big showdown for power is coming and when it does come it will be a bloody battle.' *Daily Sketch*, 30 June 1959; Draper & Challenor (D&C), p. 186; Kirby, p. 65

Page 10
'and watch every way.' Grigg, p. 32; Kirby, p. 54
'cut you up.'
'cut you up again.' Grigg, p. 32; Kirby, p. 55

Page 17
Article, redacted: JOSEPH FRANCIS OLIVA, aged 19, of 6 Ratcliffe Buildings, Bourne Estate, Clerkenwell, N. says, *Daily Sketch*, 30 June 1959; D&C, pp. 184–186; Kirby, pp. 63–65

Joe Thomas

Page 27
'A big showdown for power is coming and when it does come it will be a bloody battle.' *Daily Sketch*, 30 June 1959; D&C, p. 186; Kirby, p. 65

Page 31
'That [mad] bastard Challenor!' D&C, p. 1

Page 39
A man who [knows] no fear has nothing to conquer. D&C, p. 39

Page 41
'You're going to give us a hundred pounds or what are you going to do.'
D&C, p. 186; Kirby, p. 58

Page 43
'are you still grassing?'
'when we do up your old man' Kirby, pp. 56–57

Page 45
'Watch your drift going down. The stick is to stay as tight as possible. I will remain where I land and you are to walk to me, number six walking on to number five and so on until we pick each other up.' D&C, p. 49

Page 60
'With any luck, I'll soon be killing my first Jerry sentry.' D&C, p. 52

Page 63
'Lying on my back, smoking a cigarette and stroking her hair, I thought: what a life for a soldier!' D&C, p. 62

Page 108
'It's that bastard Gardiner; he's grassed on us. It's a nice club he's got. If he charges me, he won't have it for long.' Kirby, p. 59

Page 114
'Don't go to sleep, my [old] darling… I'm coming back.' Grigg, p. 28

Page 121
'come on… let's stripe the bastard' Grigg, p. 32; Kirby, p. 58

Page 122
'You [had] better take a barrow.' D&C, p. 63

Page 124
'It's that bastard Gardiner; he's grassed on us. It's a nice club he's got…
he won't have it for long.' Kirby, p. 59
'Can I speak to you, guv?'
'That's all right'
'I'm knackered anyway, but don't get the wrong idea. This is all a
take-on'
'Joe Oliva and a few of the boys have been taking the piss out of him'
'We wouldn't have had his money, it was just frighteners.' Grigg, p. 33;
Kirby, p. 59

Pages 127–128
'Well if it ain't fucking Oliva.'
'Arrest the two girls… in case he calls them as witnesses.' Kirby, p. 65

Page 131
'They'll never report us.'
'They daren't. What are they going to say? That they let us stroll past
without even challenging us?' D&C, p. 61

Page 133
'if I don't burn him, someone else will.' Grigg, p. 33; D&C, p. 187;
Kirby, p. 60; Morton, p. 115

Page 136
'I've eaten bigger blokes than you!' Kirby, p. 60

Page 139
'God didn't hear [you] you bastards!' D&C, p. 70

Page 140
'I suppose he put you on to me, then?'
'He doesn't know what's coming to him. He'll have to get more than you lot to look after him. His days are numbered.' D&C, p. 189; Kirby, pp. 60–61

Pages 145–146
From Judge Maude's statement on passing sentence, case of Pedrini et al, December 18, 1962; D&C, p. 183; Kirby, p. 67

Page 146
'Sergeant Harry topples "King Oliva"' *Evening Standard*, December 18, 1962; Kirby, p. 68

Page 147
'You are a spy and you will be shot if you do not help us. We want to know what you have been doing and where you have been.' D&C, p. 73

Page 148
From the *Evening News*, December 18, 1962; Kirby, p. 68

Page 153
'As a CID officer, I thought he was great. I had the greatest respect for him. He was nicking the right people at the right time.' Maurice Harding, Detective Constable, West End Central, Kirby, p. 75

Page 170
'waiting [much] longer' Grigg, p. 39

Page 173
'I've given you a chance. I could have found these in your pocket.' D&C, p. 168; Kirby, p. 74

Page 176
'I must want my head examined' Kirby, p. 74

Page 177
'Don't look any further, Sergeant. There's no jelly here. You could score all this down to aggravation. We're unlucky, that's all. That's someone else's gear.' Grigg, p. 42; D&C, pp. 168–169; Kirby, p. 74

Page 177
'I've two detonators here… I've given you a chance… I could have found these in your pockets.' D&C, p. 168; Kirby, p. 74

Page 179
'It was for someone else. This nutter was going to blast a certain speiler, right. He was going to use a nicked car with a dummy licence in case he got a pull. All I had to do was supply the necessary. The funny part about it all is that I didn't even get the dets. I was just born unlucky.' Grigg, p. 42; Kirby, p. 74

Page 188
Excerpt from *Winged Dagger*, Farran

Page 190
'May God forgive you.'
'He probably won't.' Kirby, p. 84

Page 191
'Take the black bastard out of my sight'
'I wish [I was in] in South Africa… I'd have a [redacted] for breakfast every morning.' D&C, p. 176; Morton, p. 116 ; Kirby, p. 86

Page 198
'You're fucking nicked, my old beauty.' Grigg, p. 50, Morton, p. 117, Kirby, p. 99

Page 199
'Boo the queen, would you?'
'No, not at all' D&C, p. 13, Grigg, p. 50, Kirby, p. 100

Page 200
'The biggest brick for the biggest boy.' D&C, p. 15, Grigg, p. 51, Kirby, p. 98
'Carrying an offensive weapon. You can get two years for that.' D&C, p. 14, Grigg, p. 50, Morton, p. 117, Kirby, p. 100

Acknowledgements

Arts Council England, Will Francis, Piers Russell-Cobb, Eleo Carson, Joe Harper, Rosie Stevens, Nicci Praça, Angeline Rothermundt, Kid Ethic, Laura Barton, Lee Brackstone, Luke Brown, Angus Cargill, Jake Arnott, Mick Herron, John King, Mark Timlin, Cathi Unsworth, Paul Willets, Lucy Caldwell – again! – and Martha Lecauchois, always.